MW00699010

ISBN 9781953842046

9 781953 842046

90000 >

THE SCRIBBLER FILES:

CASE OF THE MISSING MASCOT

Chris Roberts

CHRIS ROBERTS

Nudge Books

First paperback edition November 2020

Cover design by Austin Eidson

Published by Nudge Books
www.nudgebooks.com

For

Chad, Ginny, Dre, Rick, Jeff W., Rhonda, Nop, Nick, Jacob, Vinny, Dale,
Kelly, Erin, John, Genna, Whitney, JR, Natascha, Dave, Cody, TR,
Brennan, Genie, Chris ... and all the other Chart alumni.

And for Jeff B.,

who was the first to introduce me to the world of journalism.

And of course for Mr. Massa ...

a curmudgeon, but one of the best.

PROLOGUE

Chet Sayer flattened himself against the wall as lights from a passing car made shadows dance along the hallway of the broken-down house in which he was trespassing. Sooty ash-dust swirled through the light. He held his breath, hoping no one had seen his silhouette through a window. Most of the windows were smashed, with jagged pieces of glass hanging from the frames. The slight breeze that drifted in was a welcome one. Sweat beaded along Chet's forehead, both because of the heat and his nerves. It was the last day of August and the nights in Ohio were nearly as hot as the days.

The house he was exploring was one he'd been repeatedly warned to avoid by his mother and the police. But the city had recently condemned the building and scheduled it to be demolished the next day. There were ropes and taped-off doors keeping people out, but that hadn't stopped him from sneaking in. This was his last chance to examine the building and uncover the secret that had consumed his father for most of his life – a secret that had led to his mysterious death two years earlier.

Chet pulled his phone from his pocket and looked at the time. It read 11:47. It was a Friday night, and though his curfew was usually 10 p.m., this was the last Friday night of summer vacation and his mother had given him an extra two hours. He'd told her he'd be hanging out with his best friend, Justin Edwards, who lived just a few houses down. But he'd left Justin's house an hour earlier and walked the two miles to this house. He knew he'd never be able to make it home by curfew, and that meant a lecture from his mom. But for once he didn't care – any lecture he received would be worth it if he could get even one little crumb about why his father had died here. Not that he'd ever tell his mom where he'd been that night. If she found out he was looking into the same mystery that his father had, she'd lose it.

He turned to continue along the upstairs hallway, but before he took a step, he heard a noise from below. It was faint and sounded like a floorboard creaking. It made the hair on the back of his neck stand up, and he stood extremely still and listened as hard as he could for more noises. It was nearly impossible to walk through the house without making the floorboards creak – it was barely standing, after all, thanks to the fire – and Chet knew if someone else were in the house, he'd hear more creaking. After waiting a full minute without any more noises, he shrugged and let out a huff of breath. The sound must have been caused by the breeze shifting the rickety building.

The floor groaned as he continued down the hall. He wasn't a heavy boy – at age 14 he was one of the skinniest kids in his class – but his weight was enough to make the wood below him sag. He quickly moved along to avoid falling through the floor. Each step made dusty ash drift up into the air. He sneezed violently and the floorboards creaked even louder. There were holes in the floor, and he had to step carefully, easing along the edge of the hall where the foundation was strongest. Though it was dark, he could still make out the scorch marks along the walls and ceiling, where the fire had done its damage. The building was barely standing, which was why the city had condemned it and scheduled it for demolition. Chet knew he was pressing his luck by navigating the upper floors of the building, but he assumed whatever secrets the former owners of the home had kept here must have been hidden in the master bedroom.

Also … that's where his father's body had been found.

Chet honestly didn't know much about the house, nor why his father had found it so interesting in the last weeks of his life. Chet had never known much about what his father had been investigating. As a reporter for The Columbus Dispatch, his father was always digging into interesting stories. Chet had never taken much of an interest in his dad's work. He just knew that sometimes his father would get really excited about a story he was chasing and would spend many late hours in his study poring over new clues. One story in particular seemed to consume him for as long as Chet could remember – a project his father had worked on for more than a decade. And somehow the clues his father had unearthed had led him to this three-story house on the edge of town.

Chetfield was a small suburb about 60 miles east of Columbus, and this house was one of the biggest in the area. It had belonged to the town's most prominent architect – a person Chet's father had written about extensively during his time with The Columbus Dispatch. Chet knew that from digging through his father's old files. He also knew that the architect had been known around town as being extremely odd and eccentric. He collected rare artifacts and liked to build extremely difficult puzzles into his building designs – puzzles that hinted at a fabled treasure hidden somewhere in one of his many buildings. A small following of treasure-seekers around the world were enamored with the tale and made their way to Chetfield from time-to-time in hopes of unearthing some new clue in one of the architect's puzzles or enigmatic buildings.

Chet's father was not one of the treasure-seekers, though his work investigating the story for so many years had made him a familiar face in those circles. From what Chet had unearthed in his dad's notes, his father had been convinced there was something more sinister behind the architect's actions over the years. No one had believed him ... until he'd been found dead in a fire at the architect's house while the owners were away on vacation. Two years had since passed, and the local police had stopped investigating the mysterious fire long ago. It was now classified as a cold case, which was extremely frustrating to Chet. He wanted answers, and it seemed as if no one else was willing to help him find those answers – including his mother.

As Chet walked through the doorway of the master bed-room, he stopped to look around. What had once been an ornate dresser was nothing more than a few charred chunks of wood in the corner. A few other chunks of wood along the main wall showed where the bed had been, and broken glass along the opposite wall must have been a large mirror. Chet forced himself to look at the floor on the opposite corner from the dresser. That's where his father's body had been found. Though he'd not seen the body, he'd read the autopsy report and learned this his father had died by asphyxiation from smoke inhalation, with 95 percent of his body covered in third-degree burns. The only way they'd been able to identify his body had been through dental records. Chet shook his head to clear away the mental image that popped into his mind.

It didn't look like there was anything in that corner, but it was shrouded in darkness and Chet knew he'd have to go closer to get a better look. He took a deep breath and was about to walk toward it when he suddenly heard a sound again.

This time the creak of the floorboards was unmistakable … and it was upstairs! He held his breath, hoping it was just the wind again, but another creak came immediately after and there was no denying that someone else was in the house!

Chet looked around frantically, trying to think of a way out. His only option was through the window, but it was too far of a jump for him to make without seriously injuring himself. He could try to hide in the adjacent bathroom, but surely whoever was in the house would hear him if he did that.

He heard another creak behind him, and he knew he only had mere moments before the person would discover him. So, throwing caution to the wind, he jumped toward the window. But at the last second a thought came to him, and he reached down and grabbed a piece of the charred wood and threw it out the window before darting through the bathroom door. There was a large porcelain tub sitting in the corner, and Chet jumped into it and laid himself flat on his back. A puff of ash dust billowed around him and he held his hand over his nose to muffle a sneeze. A second later he heard the chunk of wood he'd thrown hit the ground below the window with a loud *CLACK*!

Chet struggled to breathe quietly, even though he was panting with fear. He waited, hoping against hope that the person in the hallway wouldn't discover him and would instead assume the sound outside was from him jumping out the window. A moment later he heard the floorboards creak inside the master bedroom. He listened as the person made his or her way toward the window. Who could it be? A police officer? Had someone seen him sneak into the house?

The creaking stopped, and Chet imagined the person looking out the window at the ground below. It was very dark outside, so there was a good chance the person wouldn't be able to see much on the ground – especially since there were so many trees set close to the house.

It seemed like an eternity before Chet heard a sound again, and when he did it startled him so badly that he gave a violent flinch that made his shoe scrape against the edge of the tub and give off a faint squeak. Chet froze and strained to listen, hoping the other person hadn't heard the noise his foot had made. The floorboards groaned as the other person continued to walk away from the window, and it sounded like whoever it was hadn't noticed him as they continued away from the bathroom.

Chet counted to 30, then slowly peeked his head up over the lip of the bathtub. It was dark, but his eyes had adjusted well and he could see holes in the wall caused by the fire. Moonlight filtering through the window also helped. Through one of the holes he could make out the shape of a person, though he couldn't tell if it was a man or a woman. The person was facing away from him and had made his or her way toward the corner of the room where Chet's father's body had been found. The person stooped down and examined the floor and walls and started doing something with the boards on the wall, though Chet couldn't see what it was. A second later the person pulled back hard on the wood of the wall and a loud *crack* made Chet jump. He accidentally banged his head against the edge of the tub with a dull thud. The person froze and cocked his or her head as if listening for something. Chet ducked back down immediately and rubbed his head.

A moment later another loud *crack* indicated that the person was continuing to pull boards from the wall, and Chet wondered what he or she was looking for. The *cracks* continued for another few minutes before stopping suddenly. Chet slowly eased his head up again to get another look. The person was standing, and though it was very dark it looked as if he or she was holding something. Chet inhaled sharply in despair, breathing in a small dust cloud of ash. He couldn't stop himself from sneezing, and the person turned and looked directly at him. There was just enough light coming through the window that Chet could see the whites of the person's eyes. Whomever it was seemed shocked, and immediately took off running.

Chet jumped out of the tub and darted into the room, chasing after the person. He didn't know what the person had found in the corner, but he was convinced it had something to do with his father's mystery and he wasn't about to let someone else run away with such a valuable piece of information. He could hear the person scrambling down the stairs, and just as he was about to turn the corner and follow, he heard a terrible crunching sound. The floor began to shake and the stairs began to fall apart. The person wasn't quite to the bottom of the stairs yet and had to jump to avoid falling through as they crumbled beneath. Whomever it was landed awkwardly and let out a yelp of pain. The voice made Chet think it was a man, and it looked as if he'd sprained his ankle. The stranger groaned and slowly pulled himself up to his feet, favoring his leg. He turned and glared up at Chet, then stumbled out through the front door.

Chet desperately wanted to follow, but he knew it was a terrible idea to try to jump down. As if confirming that, the stairs completely collapsed and started taking parts of the floor with them. He scrambled back as the floorboards in the hallway began to break off and fall into the floor below. The house began to shake, and pieces of the ceiling began to break off and rain down around him. The more pieces that broke apart, the faster everything seemed to disintegrate … and the closer and closer he came to being buried in rubble.

Chet looked frantically for a way out, but there was no way to get back to the bottom floor. He considered jumping through one of the holes, but he worried he'd sprain an ankle like the other man had, or twist a knee and end up with the building collapsing on top of him. He rushed back down the hall, jumping over holes and dancing along the edges where the floorboards were the strongest. He made his way to another room at the very end of the hall and peeked in. There was a fireplace in this room, with broken windows on either side of the chimney. Chet rushed over to one of the windows and looked out. Just as he'd hoped, there was ivy growing up along the side of the chimney on the outside of the building. He'd have to stretch far, but Chet was fairly certain he could reach it.

He started to ease himself out of the window and then heard another loud crash from behind. When he looked back he was consumed by a huge cloud of ash that burst out the window around him. He assumed the hallway had completely collapsed, which meant the room he was in wasn't far behind. Desperately he reached around the edge of the window and stretched for the ivy on the chimney. He didn't feel anything but air, so he stretched harder, straining more than he'd ever had to strain in his life. Just as he felt the floor fall out from under his foot his hand grasped a thick vein of ivy and he leaped out the window, dangling from vegetation that was slowly starting to tear away.

Another burst of ash exited the window as he clung desperately to the ivy. He looked down and saw that he wasn't too far from the ground, though still far enough that if he let go he'd hurt himself. Very carefully he eased himself down, holding as tightly as he could to the ivy. More and more of the vegetation pulled away from the wall and he scrambled frantically for a better handhold. The ivy provided just enough support for him to climb about halfway down before it gave way completely from the wall. With a grunt he squeezed his eyes shut and kicked off from the chimney, dropping to the ground.

The jolt was abrupt, but it wasn't enough to give him more than a minor ache in his knees and ankles. He looked up at the window he'd just climbed from and frowned. More loud crashes were coming from inside the building and the roof was sagging lower and lower with every passing moment. Chet backed away from the building and then started looking around for the person he'd been chasing. There was no sign of someone else, and Chet's heart sank. Whatever the person had found had seemed small – it certainly wasn't a treasure chest. He'd been so close to getting a new clue about his father's death, but now someone else had run off with it. And there was no going back into the house to look for more clues.

As if to confirm that thought, the house gave one last large shudder and then completely collapsed on itself. A huge bloom of ash puffed into the air and Chet was forced to back away even farther. He stood and stared in disappointment for a long time. It was as if the last nail in his father's coffin had shut him away from any understanding of the mystery.

After a long, quiet moment he pulled his phone out of his pocket and looked at the time. It was 12:09. There were two messages from his mother on his phone. His heart sank even more as he anticipated the scolding he'd get for being late.

He gave one last forlorn look at the architect's house, then lowered his head and started walking home. Each step away from the building was like another shovel-full of dirt on his father's grave, and by the time he'd made his way home he'd buried the mystery deep down. His freshman year of high school started next week and he was looking forward to a new chapter of his life. His father's mystery didn't have a place in that life, so he let it go. It was one of the hardest things he'd ever done in his life. But it would have to stay a mystery, and he'd have to learn to be OK with that.

CHAPTER 1

THE LEGEND OF CHUNK AND CHET

The last Saturday of summer vacation was one of the hottest days ever recorded in Ohio history. The humidity was particularly thick – so bad that Chet felt like he could reach out and squeeze the air itself and drops of water would fall to the ground.

He hadn't slept well the night before – too many thoughts of what he'd experienced and who the strange man might be – so he wasn't feeling great when he arrived at the high school football practice. He wasn't there to participate in team activities. He'd been assigned his first story for the school newspaper – The Scribbler – and was at the practice field in hopes of getting an interview. He wanted to make a good impression on his adviser, Dr. Delmar. So, when the teacher had suggested he visit the practice on Saturday, Chet had grudgingly agreed. He considered it a waste of time, especially since the person he'd been sent to interview didn't seem to be there, but he was going through the motions just to prove to his adviser that he could be a good and thorough reporter.

He was also there because he didn't want to be at home right now. His mother was furious with him, and the frosty silence that existed between them was extremely uncomfortable. He'd known his mom was going to be mad when he arrived an hour later than curfew, but he'd underestimated just how disappointed she was when she realized where he'd been. It was a little hard to deny that he'd gone exploring the architect's house considering he was covered in ash, and when his mom had seen him, her face had dissolved into such a mixture of disappointment and anger that Chet had wanted to bury his head in the ground. She'd barely said two words to him today, and when she'd dropped him off at the football field, she'd given him a curt, "I'll pick you up in two hours. Be ready to go when I get here."

He tried not to dwell on it, and instead concentrated on what was happening on the football field. Players were separated into different squads – Chet assumed it was position groups – and were doing various drills. Chet could see his best friend, Justin – better known by his nickname Chunk – on the far end zone practicing goal-line formations. He felt a moment of pity for his friend because of the heat. If Chet was dying of thirst, Chunk must be parched.

Chet started to make his way around the field and then noticed a police car pull up. Two officers got out of their vehicle and started walking toward him. Chet wiped his forehead with the sleeve of his t-shirt and stared uncertainly at the two officers. He pulled his wet shirt away from his neck and tried not to panic as thoughts of going to jail flew through his mind. He was certain they were there for him, but suddenly they took a slight turn and walked directly to the head coach.

One of the officers shook the coach's hand. The players on the field stopped practicing and stared at the officers. Chet eased closer to try and hear what they were talking about.

"Hi Irv," said one of the officers, addressing the head coach. "Have you seen Gavin Brigantz today?"

A wave of intense curiosity washed over Chet. *Who was Gavin Brigantz?*

"No," the coach said. "Haven't seen him since Thursday's practice. Why?"

"His mother called us this morning saying her son didn't come home last night," the officer replied. "He was supposed to stay with his father Thursday night after practice, but his father doesn't remember seeing him – not that his statement is reliable considering how drunk he was. You know how Eddie Brigantz can get."

The coach nodded his head and frowned. Chet assumed

Gavin's parents must be divorced and that he split time between two homes. A twinge of pity seeped in as he considered how awful it must be for Gavin to have an alcoholic for a father.

At least his father is still alive, Chet thought callously.

"Anyway, he hasn't been seen since Thursday night," the officer continued. "It's been nearly 48 hours since anyone has last seen him. Do you by chance recall what time he left here Thursday?"

The coach turned to his other coaches, and a couple of them shrugged their shoulders in a non-committal way. He turned back and shrugged, as well.

"Well, practice ended late that day," the coach said. "I'd say maybe 8 p.m. It was our second-to-last practice before the school year, so I was running the boys a little harder than normal. I'm pretty sure the Brigantz boy left right after practice was over."

Chet scribbled on his notepad the time "8 p.m." and began sketching out a timeline with locations. He wasn't sure why he did it, other than an instinct that he might need it later.

"Any idea where he might have gone?" the officer asked.

The coach shook his head.

Chet was suddenly startled by a girl standing next to him. She was staring intently at the officers, but had come right up to Chet's shoulder and leaned in close, whispering in his ear.

"Did I hear them say something about Gavin Brigantz?" the girl asked. She was an upperclassman and had a somewhat stocky build, with short-cropped black hair and black glasses. She was wearing a belt that had two water bottles in pockets on the sides. There were hand towels tucked into each of her back pockets. He assumed she was a team manager. Like Chet, she was sweating.

"Yeah," he answered. "Do you know him?"

"Yes," she answered simply, not taking her eyes from the officers.

"Well … do you know where he is?" Chet pressed.

"No … which is kind of strange," she said, eyebrows forming a V on her forehead as she frowned. "I haven't heard from him for two days!"

"So, you're friends?" Chet asked.

"He's my *best* friend," the girl corrected, finally turning away from the officers long enough to give Chet a withering look. "I tried messaging him like 10 times today, but he hasn't answered any of my texts. I tried to call and message him last night, too, but he didn't answer."

"Huh," Chet said. "Maybe he's sick or something."

The girl looked at him skeptically.

"He's so sick that he doesn't answer his messages?" she asked.

"Well, I dunno," Chet said. "What're you thinking?"

17

"I'm not thinking anything," she said angrily. "Just wondering where my friend is."

"Ah," Chet said, wracking his brain for something else to say. "I'm Chet, by the way."

"Chet?" she said, looking at him again, this time with skepticism on her face. "Is that a joke?"

"No," Chet said flatly, his face reddening. "It's just a coincidence."

"It's just a coincidence that your name is Chet and you go to school at Chetfield High School?" the girl said, a sarcastic laugh escaping her lips. "Good luck with that, freshman. You're gonna have a fun first day of school."

Chet winced. Chunk had warned him of this – that his name would be the butt of many jokes during the first few weeks of school – but Chet had hoped his friend's exaggerations would be unfounded. Apparently, he was wrong.

"What's your name?" Chet asked, reaching for something to change the subject.

"Jess," she said crisply.

"How do you know Gavin?" Chet asked.

"We've been friends since sixth grade," she said, obviously impatient with his questions. "I started as team manager when he became school mascot last year. We hang out all the time."

"Wait, Gavin is the school mascot?!" Chet blurted out –

so loudly that the officers and coaches turned toward him. Sweat trickled down the side of his face as everyone's eyes were on him.

"Did something bad happen to him?" Jess suddenly asked, taking a step toward the officers. There was a worried expression on her face. "You know, like a car crash or something. Though you'd think I would have heard about that. His mom knows we're best friends. It's just weird. I mean, he always answers his messages …"

The officer blinked, then frowned.

"How do you know Gavin, young lady?" the officer asked.

"He's my best friend," Jess said. "Please … what's going on?"

"Have you heard from him at any time between now and last Thursday?" the officer pressed.

"No!" Jess said, practically yelling. "He won't answer any of my messages! What happened to him? You have to find him!"

"We're working on it," the officer replied, putting his hands up in a gesture clearly meant to be pacifying. "It would help if you could give us any idea where he might have gone. Where does he hang out? Do you know if he was going to meet anybody? Did he say anything about leaving town?"

Jess's face was filled with emotion, and she reached up hastily with her right hand and wiped away a tear that had started to leak down her cheek.

"I … I don't know," she stammered, wiping away another tear. The officer looked around at the coaches and players who were staring at them, then seemed to take pity on her.

"Would you mind coming to the station and answering some questions?" he asked gently, holding out a hand to her.

Jess took control of her emotions and nodded. The officers walked with her back to the parking lot next to the football field, and moments later Jess was riding away from the field in the back of a police car.

It took a moment for the shock to wear off on everyone gathered on the field. The players were starting to whisper to each other.

"Five-minute break!" the coach yelled suddenly, making everyone jump.

Immediately the players rushed to a long table on the sideline that held five large orange water jugs. One of the boys lagged at the back, not running at all, and the coach yelled at him to "move your butt!"

"Why do coaches have to be so mean?" Chet wondered out loud to himself.

"Probably because nice coaches don't win games," a voice said at Chet's shoulder, causing him to jump.

"Sheesh Chunk!" Chet exclaimed. "Scared me to death!"

Chunk just laughed and clapped Chet on the shoulder. He winced. Sometimes Chunk didn't realize his strength.

"What're you doing here?" Chunk asked. "I thought for sure you'd be grounded after going to that house last night."

"Well … you promise not to laugh?"

"No way. If it's something embarrassing to you, then I am definitely going to laugh."

Chet snorted. "Some friend you are."

"Only the best," Chunk said. "Somebody has to keep you humble, right? Let me guess: It has something to do with a newspaper story or something."

Chet gave Chunk a sour look and then nodded. "Yeah, I have to do a story on the school mascot."

True to his word, Chunk laughed – loudly. Chunk was already a loud individual – he ate loud and talked loud and walked loud and did just about everything loud. But the thing he did the loudest was laugh, and at that moment his laugh was loud enough to catch the attention of the group of coaches standing not far away.

"Hey, Edwards!" the head coach said, pointing at Chunk. "Break is over! Get your butt back on the field."

"OK Coach," Chunk replied immediately. "I think Chet needs to ask you something about Charlie the Chicken hawk though!"

Chunk yelled that last bit so as many people around them could hear, and it did the trick as most of those within hearing distance immediately started snickering – including a couple of the coaches. Chet blushed in embarrassment, but plucked up the courage to walk toward the group of coaches.

"Thanks … jerk," he said to Chunk over his shoulder as he walked away.

"Anytime," Chunk replied, laughing again.

Chet walked up to the head coach. He was tall and lean with a weathered face and sun burnt skin. He raised an eyebrow at Chet as he approached.

"What do you need, son?" the coach asked, perturbed. "We're in the middle of practice here."

"Sorry, er … sir," Chet said. "Dr. Delmar said I need to do a story on the school mascot. He just said to show up at practice today and ask around."

Chet shrugged and looked up at the coach. He was hoping there was at least a little compassion in the man. Though his father's death had hardened him to the world, Chet still believed in the basic goodness of most people.

"So, Edwards wasn't making a joke?" the coach asked, his face softening as he offered Chet a small smile. "You really do want to ask me something about the school mascot?"

"Er, yeah," Chet replied lamely. "I didn't even know who it was until a few minutes ago. So … he's really missing?"

The coach looked at him for a long moment, as if weighing the wisdom of talking to a freshman student about a police investigation. Then he half-shrugged to himself as if to say, *What's the harm?*

"Well, obviously Brigantz isn't here," he said. "He was supposed to be, and he didn't show up. I don't know where he is. Last I saw him was at Thursday's practice."

"Oh ... OK," Chet said, shrinking back.

"Is that it?" the coach asked, half turning toward the other coaches and beginning to dismiss Chet from his mind.

"Actually," Chet said, "is there anything interesting you can tell me about the mascot?"

The coach turned back to Chet and gave him a frown. Chet knew it was a lame question, but he'd lobbed it out there desperately hoping to get some kind of a quote from the coach.

"The mascot?" he asked, seeming truly surprised that Chet would ask him about something so ridiculous. Chet wished he could have taken the words back. "That stupid chicken hawk is the least of my worries. I'm trying to win a state championship this year. If Brigantz can't keep track of his Halloween costume, it's not my fault."

"Right ... sorry – wait, what?" Chet said, trying to organize his thoughts as he replayed in his mind what the coach had just said. "Is the costume missing or something?"

"I don't know," the coach shrugged indifferently, the compassion from a moment ago now completely evaporated. "And frankly, I don't care. And no, you cannot quote me on that."

"No, of course not," Chet replied immediately. "But … um … you just said, 'If Brigantz can't keep track of his Halloween costume, it's not your fault.' What did you mean by that?"

The coach let out a heavy sigh.

"The costume is always stored in the locker in my office," he said, clearly disinterested in Chet's story assignment. "It wasn't there today. I assumed Brigantz didn't show up this morning because he'd forgotten it at home or something and had to go back for it. He doesn't have a car – he just rides his bike everywhere. But he didn't show up after lunch, either, so maybe something else happened."

"Oh," Chet said, not knowing what else to ask.

"Are we done here?" the coach asked with a small scowl. "Would it be alright with you if I go do my job?"

The coach's sarcasm was not wasted on Chet, who nodded vigorously and backed away. As the coach made his way back to the others, Chet lingered on the sideline and wondered what to do next. He wandered around the field aimlessly, thinking about Gavin's disappearance and trying not to let thoughts of the night before creep into his mind. He started to think about the story he would write for The Scribbler and decided that the case of the missing mascot made for a pretty interesting first assignment after all. It was just the sort of story his dad would have chased down. It was during new experiences, like heading to high school as a freshman, that Chet most missed his dad and the calm wisdom he provided.

When practice finally ended, Chet joined Chunk as he marched to the locker room. He had about 10 minutes before his mom would pick him up, and he wanted to talk to Chunk more about Gavin. Two other boys from the team were walking with him. They were on the offensive line with Chunk and were pretty big, though not quite as big as Chet's best friend. Chunk was abnormally large for a freshman, and his athleticism already had people talking about his chances to play Division I football after graduation. Chet quickly learned that the two boys were seniors and starters for the varsity team – Kevin Beckweth and Steve Charles. Apparently, Chunk had made an impression on them.

"What was all that about with the cops?" Chunk asked as Chet walked up to them.

"Apparently Gavin Brigantz has gone missing," Chet replied. "He's the guy I was supposed to talk to about the mascot."

"Gavin is missing?!" one of the other boys – Kevin – asked.

"That's what the officer said," Chet replied. "Hasn't been seen since Thursday night, apparently."

Kevin and Steve shared a look that Chet couldn't quite decipher.

"What?" Chet asked immediately. "Do you know something?"

"No … not really," Kevin said.

"Not really?" Chet asked. "Sounds like you know something."

Kevin and Steve shared another look, and Kevin kind of winced.

"He's just … not the easiest guy to get along with," Steve said. "He just takes things too far, you know? He never knows when to stop pushing peoples' buttons."

Kevin nodded at that, obviously agreeing with Steve's assessment. Chet wasn't sure what else to ask, so he remained silent as he continued walking with them up the hill to the locker rooms.

"Hey Chunk, I'm not gonna be able to come over later," Chet said. "My mom is pretty angry about last night. If it hadn't been for a school assignment she never would have let me come here today."

Before Chunk could answer, Kevin and Steve burst out laughing.

"Wait … Chunk?!" Kevin asked, laughing. "Like from 'The Goonies?'"

"Ha! Yes!" Chunk replied. "Chet gave me that nickname back in seventh grade!"

Chunk clapped Chet on the shoulder, making him wince. It really hurt when he hit him like that.

"Why?" Steve asked, still chuckling.

"I wasn't thinking, actually," Chet said hesitantly. "I just kind of blurted it out while we were doing in-house suspension together."

"You both got suspended?!" Kevin asked, skeptical but now fully interested.

"Yeah," Chet said, shrugging uncomfortably.

"Yeah?! That's it? C'mon, you gotta give us more than that!" Kevin said, pushing for them to tell the story.

"I moved here in seventh grade," Chunk said. "I didn't know anybody, so when I saw Chet walking past my house on the first day, headed to the bus stop, I hurried out and started walking with him."

"I couldn't believe it," Chet said. "Nobody really talked to me in seventh grade. I was kind of a nerd."

"You still are," Chunk said playfully, clapping him on the shoulder while Kevin and Steve laughed.

"Yeah, well, most people picked on me back then, so it was a total shock when someone as cool as Chunk started talking to me," Chet said. "Then we got on the bus and Duncan Cline started being a jerk. He's the worst. Always used to punch me as hard as he could in my arm every time we had gym class together. Said it was his way of making me tougher. He'd sit behind me in class and flick my ear. Anything he could do to try to hurt me, he'd do it. That's what he started doing on the bus that morning. My dad had just ... well, I'd had a pretty rough summer, so it was really bothering me, even though usually I just try to ignore it."

"I could tell Chet was getting really angry," Chunk said, continuing the story. "But he didn't say or do anything the entire ride to school, which I thought was pretty cool. I could see his face and I knew he was holding back his anger with everything he had. Most guys don't have that kind of self-control. Anyway, when we got to school Chet jumped up and tried to get off the bus as fast as he could, but Duncan reached out his foot and tripped Chet. He fell on his face – *BAM*! I couldn't stand it any longer. So, while Duncan was laughing, I turned around and punched him in his big fat nose."

"You did?!" Kevin asked.

"That's awesome!" Steve added.

"It was awesome," Chet said, not bothering to conceal his grin. "I didn't see it, but I heard it. Sounded like a big, wet *crunch*! I turned around and saw Duncan holding his face, and bright red blood was everywhere!"

"Yes!" Kevin said, pumping his fist into the air triumphantly. Steve just laughed while nodding at Chunk affirmatively.

"Yeah, well, we ended up getting in-house suspension for fighting," Chunk said. "We were supposed to do homework that day, but we just spent the day talking about our favorite movies. Chet told me his dad's favorite movie was 'The Goonies,' and then he blurted out that I looked just like Chunk. The name pretty much stuck ever since."

"I love it!" Kevin said. "That's totally your nickname now. We're putting that on your jersey."

"No way Coach Smith will let that happen," Steve retorted skeptically.

"I bet he will," Kevin replied.

"Ten dollars says he won't."

"Done," Kevin replied, spitting on his hand and holding it out to Steve, who also spit on his hand and shook Kevin's hand.

"Gambling on sports, eh?" Chunk said with a grin. "I'm pretty sure that's illegal, guys."

"Oh, shut up," Kevin said with a smile, playfully punching Chunk in the arm. "Besides, that's just a little bet. If you really want to see some gambling, you should come to our poker game this Friday night."

"Poker?" Chunk asked. "Like, with real money?"

"Yeah!" Steve said. "That reminds me … a couple weeks ago Gavin won 100 dollars!"

"Wait, Gavin?" Chet asked without thinking. "The same Gavin we were just talking about?"

Both boys laughed.

"Yep," Kevin said. "He's always at those poker games."

"He wasn't there last night, though," Steve said thoughtfully. "Good thing, too, because I actually walked away with some money for once!"

Kevin laughed at him.

"Could we, uh … come next week?" Chet asked.

"You sure your mom will let you go?" Chunk asked, and Chet's heart immediately sank.

"Oh yeah," he said flatly. "I forgot."

"Just tell her it's for a newspaper assignment," Chunk said.

Chet looked at his friend uncertainly, but then nodded and looked back at Kevin expectantly. The two boys looked at each other, and Steve shrugged his shoulders as if to say: *Why not?*

"Yeah, sure," Kevin said. "We'd be glad to take your money. Starts at 8 p.m. Bring 20 bucks."

Chet smiled. "Thanks!"

"No, thank you," Kevin said, laughing again. "You're what we'd call in the poker world a 'dead fish.' We'll be happy to relieve you of your cash!"

Both senior boys started laughing, and Chunk joined them. Chet lowered his head in embarrassment and let them continue on into the locker room while he turned and made his way back to the parking lot to meet his mom.

CHS Senior Gavin Brigantz Missing

Student who portrays school mascot declared an official missing person by police

By Chet Sayer
The Scribbler · Reporter

A Chetfield High School student has been officially declared missing by the Chetfield Police Department, and a state-wide search is underway for his whereabouts.

Gavin Brigantz was last seen leaving the high school football field Thursday evening following the team's practice. Brigantz is the student tabbed to inhabit the Charlie the Chicken hawk mascot suit this year, and as such is often involved with various team activities in and around the school. Head Football Coach Irv Smith said he saw Brigantz get on his bike following the practice, and others confirm that he was seen riding away. Gavin's parents are divorced, and his mother claims her son was supposed to spend the night with his father. But Gavin's father, Eddie Brigantz, told officers his son never came to his house.

"The investigation into the disappearance of Gavin Brigantz has expanded into a state-wide search," said Police Chief Matt Williams. "There is no reason, at this point, to fear any foul play is at hand. However, we aren't ruling anything out. If anyone has any knowledge or information as to Gavin's whereabouts, or of his activities on the night of his disappearance, we strongly encourage you to come forward."

Principal Bill Miller has announced that he and the rest of the school staff will work in full cooperation with authorities to help re-create Brigantz's movements in the days and moments leading up to his last known whereabouts. Principal Miller also said the duties associated with performing as Charlie the Chicken hawk would be temporarily put on hold, as opposed to handed to someone else, in the event of Brigantz's return.

Perhaps related to Brigantz's disappearance, the Charlie costume has also gone missing. According to Coach Smith, the costume is usually kept in the storage locker in his office. He recalls Brigantz taking it out of the locker prior to last Thursday's practice, but said he can't recall having seen it anywhere around his office or the football team's locker room in the days since.

"I have no idea what happened to it," Coach Smith said. "That stupid costume is the least of my worries. I'm trying to win a state championship this year. I'm truly sorry that Gavin has gone missing and I join everyone else in praying that nothing bad has happened to him. That said, if he can't keep track of his costume, that's his own fault."

Principal Miller said he encourages any students who might have knowledge of anything having to do with Brigantz to share that information with school counselors. He also said anyone found to have tampered with or destroyed the Charlie costume will be punished with severity – up to and including expulsion.

CHAPTER 2

THE FIRST PITCH MEETING

Chet smiled proudly as he finished reading the article he'd written about Gavin. He couldn't help feeling a smug sense of accomplishment at having finished the story so quickly. He'd worked hard over the weekend and even contacted Dr. Delmar late Sunday evening to see about posting the story on The Scribbler's website by Monday morning. Dr. Delmar had personally edited the article – something he usually left to the upperclassmen who served as editors of the paper – so that Chet's story could be released on the first day of school.

The Scribbler was CHS's award-winning online and print publication. It was run by students under the supervision of Dr. Delmar. Almost all of the students on staff were upperclassmen, with few exceptions. Chet happened to be one of those exceptions, and he was thrilled to have landed such a strong story with his first assignment out of the gate. He loved news and was especially interested in the news presented by The Scribbler because it was about to become his new "home" for the next four years.

"Home" … that was the word he associated with the high school newsroom. As a freshman, he was equal parts nervous and excited about the new school he was attending – but when it came to his newspaper class there was no fear whatsoever. He'd been looking forward to being a newspaper reporter for the past two years and was eager to begin his time with The Scribbler.

It was the first day of his freshman year. He'd already had five classes that day, as well as lunch, and the class he'd been looking forward to the most had finally arrived. Freshman year was notoriously boring when it came to classes because most freshmen didn't get to choose classes they'd really enjoy. But everyone got to choose one elective – from band to art to VoTech – and Chet had chosen newspaper/yearbook. The best part was that the class came at the end of the day, which meant every day could end on a high note.

But when Chet walked through the doors of the newspaper room at CHS for the second time in his life – having been there the week before for the pre-school-year meeting – he was underwhelmed. The lackluster room was nondescript, to say the least – mostly white walls with only one cork board that featured faded clippings of old newspapers.

There also weren't any students in the room – no buzz of activity and no reporters tossing ideas to one another. None of the computers were open, let alone being typed upon. And worst of all, it was quiet ... the wrong kind of quiet. He almost wished they still used typewriters, so the clatter of keys would fill the room with activity. He wanted to yell or stomp or clap his hands to make some kind of noise because it just felt weird.

He didn't do any of those things. Instead, he dropped his backpack onto the nearest chair, which made enough of a noise that he felt satisfied. Then he walked over to the wall on the far side of the room and looked at the newspaper clippings. There were eight of them on the board, and Chet was impressed with how the design and style of the paper had evolved over the years. Though The Scribbler was primarily an online publication today, it still printed a small run of papers that were distributed to students and alumni. The design of the paper at present was ultra-sleek and modern minimalist, with plenty of white space and bold photos. That was quite a bit different from the Word Art of the 1990s or the crowded and linear look of the 2000s. But the legacy of the newspaper and the journey it had taken over the years was not lost on Chet in that moment. It was enough to help him shake off the underwhelming feeling he'd had upon entering the room, and he felt a slow smile creep onto his face as he began to dream about the part he would play in the continuing legacy of this paper over the next four years.

When Chet turned around, there was a girl standing in

the room. She was staring at him, and Chet's first thought was that she was pretty. She had long black hair that was pulled away from her face with a wide hair band, and it fell down to her shoulders in a way that framed her face. She wore glasses – black-rimmed with purple butterflies on the stems. There was a very light dusting of freckles on her nose, which was just slightly big for her face but not in an off-putting way – more pointy than wide. Her lips *were* wide, though, and when she saw that Chet had noticed her, she broke into a big smile. Her smile was beautiful.

"Hi," the girl said, hesitating and then taking a step toward him. "I'm Kaiah."

Chet shook his head slightly to bring himself back to reality, then smiled back at her.

"Chet," he said in response. "I'm a freshman."

"Me too," Kaiah said. "Wait … Chet?! You're the one who wrote the Gavin Brigantz story! You're a freshman?!"

Chet smiled widely and couldn't help standing a little straighter.

"Yep!" he said proudly.

"Nice work!" Kaiah said. "How'd you do that so fast?"

"Well … it was my assignment from last week," Chet said, "though I did get a little bit lucky by being in the right place at the right time."

"Aw dang it!" Kaiah said, slamming her backpack down

on the table next to Chet's. "I knew I was going to miss something big at last week's meeting! What other good stories got assigned that I missed out on?!"

Chet frowned at her, wondering who she was. He'd been a student in the Chetfield School District from the time he was in kindergarten, and as such he was familiar with – or at least had seen the faces of – every other student in the district. But he'd never seen Kaiah before, so he was surprised that she, a fellow freshman, would have been given special permission to be on The Scribbler staff. He also was curious why she would have missed a meeting as important as the pre-school-year meeting. It was mandatory for all freshmen allowed into the journalism class.

"I'm guessing you're new to the school …" Chet said.

"Yeah, my family moved here from Seattle over the summer," Kaiah said, rolling her eyes.

"Why would you move from Seattle to Ohio?!" Chet blurted without thinking.

Kaiah chuckled and smiled. Chet discovered in that moment that getting Kaiah to smile would become one of his favorite things to do over the next four years.

"My dad got a job here," she said with a shrug. "He got laid off like a year ago and had been having a hard time finding a new job. He finally found one here and so we moved …"

She shrugged again as she finished, as if to say she didn't know what else to say and that she wasn't entirely comfortable with being in a new place. Chet had pity on her and tried to change the subject.

"So, you're in the newspaper class, too?"

"Yep!" she said, the smile coming back full force. "I was editor of the middle school paper at my old school."

"Me too!" Chet said, truly impressed. "That's cool! I'm gonna be editor here someday."

"Not if I beat you to it," Kaiah replied, her wide smile slipping into more of a sly one, and her eyes dancing with a mixture of mirth and challenge. "Though it looks like I'm gonna have to play catchup already. I can't believe you got such a big story right out of the gate! Seriously impressive."

"Thanks!" Chet said, unable and unwilling to wipe the huge smile from his face.

Just then four more students walked into the classroom. Three of them were boys, and the fourth was a girl. Her name was Elizabeth Cho and she was the managing editor of the paper. That meant she was second-in-command, after the editor-in-chief, Sam Chapin. He was the tall boy of the group. He shot Chet a dirty look for some reason, but then pointedly ignored him. Chet could only surmise that Sam was unhappy Chet had superseded his authority by going straight to Dr. Delmar for the Gavin Brigantz story.

Elizabeth was short – something that was put into stark relief next to Sam's height – and she had features that Chet automatically assumed were of Asian heritage. She didn't look like she smiled much, and when her eyes landed on Chet, he almost flinched back at the disdain behind them. She obviously wasn't happy with him, either.

The other two boys were named Jim and Caleb – two other seniors who were Sam's best friends. They were sports reporters for the paper, and Chet assumed they were probably angry with him, too. They didn't give him a second look, however, as they were engaged in a heated debate with Sam about whether or not the CHS football team had a chance to make the state championship this year. Their debate was loud, and it immediately cut off Kaiah and Chet's conversation.

"There's no WAY we're gonna win this year," Sam said emphatically. "Coach is gonna make Aaron quarterback, and he can't throw an accurate pass more than 20 yards to save his life!"

"Who cares?" Jim said. He was slightly shorter and stockier than Sam, and he had a big jawline. "We don't need him to throw the ball. Our running game is better than any other school in Ohio!"

"He's right," said Caleb, the smallest of the bunch. He had bright red hair and freckles all over his face and arms. "We can run the ball against anybody. Who's gonna stop us?"

"Pickering," Sam said confidently, referring to one of the biggest high schools in the state.

Neither of the other two boys responded, and when they

looked at each other it was obvious Sam had made a valid point.

"OK, I'll give you that," Jim said. "They can probably stop the run … but I still think we can beat them. Aaron isn't that bad of a quarterback!"

Chet stopped paying attention to the rest of their conversation as other students started arriving. Every one of them was older than him and Kaiah, and it was quickly apparent that they were the only two freshmen in the class. That wasn't unusual, as most spots on the newspaper staff were reserved for upperclassmen who had put in the work in various English classes and earned their way onto the team. Usually the only freshmen allowed onto the newspaper staff were those who – like Chet – received a recommendation from the junior high adviser, or who received special permission from a school counselor. Apparently, Kaiah was one of the latter, and that made sense considering she'd been editor of the newspaper at her previous school. Chet wondered idly if she was going to be a roadblock to his rise toward becoming editor of the paper someday. Part of him looked forward to the challenge.

An unspoken agreement passed between him and Kaiah in that moment, and the two of them chose seats together. The desks in the newsroom weren't set up in a traditional classroom setting. Instead of rows, the desks were set up in circles, with a bank of surge protectors and power cords in the center of each pod. Chet and Kaiah found themselves at a pod with two girls that Chet assumed were juniors or seniors. The fifth chair at the pod was empty.

A minute later the newspaper adviser, Dr. Delmar, walked into the room. Though he'd guided many of The Scribbler's newspaper staff to awards over the years, the old man was nearing the end of his career as a teacher. Chet assumed his would be the last graduating class for Dr. Delmar before he retired, and he wasn't sure how he felt about that. Word was that Dr. Delmar had lost his passion for teaching after his wife of 35 years had passed away from cancer a year before. Chet didn't like to judge people on rumors, however, so he decided to give the old man the benefit of the doubt and wait to see what kind of teacher he would be. Besides, his experience with the aging man had been fairly positive over the past week.

"Hi everyone," Dr. Delmar said, addressing the class. "Welcome to a new year at good ole CHS! Welcome back to most of you, and to our new recruits, welcome officially to The Scribbler!"

All eyes swung to Chet and Kaiah, and Chet felt his face flush with slight embarrassment. But most of the people in the class smiled at him encouragingly.

"If you all weren't paying attention last week, this is Chet Sayer," Dr. Delmar said, nodding slightly toward Chet. "He's kicked things off with quite a bang, I'd say. Wouldn't you all agree? I don't know if I've ever heard of a freshman landing such a big story at all in the history of The Scribbler, let alone before school even officially started! I must say, well done Chet!"

Dr. Delmar bestowed Chet with a fond smile, and the girls who were sitting at the table with him smiled and gave him respectful nods. Chet noticed across the room that Sam and the others with him weren't smiling. In fact, almost all of them had their arms crossed and were staring daggers at him.

Yep, Chet thought to himself, *they're definitely not happy.*

As if to confirm his inner thoughts, Caleb snorted and shook his head.

"I suppose we should call you Lord Chetfield now?" the red-haired boy quipped with an evil grin on his face. A few of the students in the classroom snickered at the comment, and Chet felt his face flush in embarrassment.

Chunk's warnings about the jokes had been, unfortunately, very accurate. In every single class he'd had that day the other kids had laughed at him when his name had been called by the teacher taking attendance. Caleb's quip merely joined the flock of others Chet had endured that day. Thankfully, Dr. Delmar took pity on him and immediately changed the subject by introducing Kaiah to the group.

"This is Kaiah Dufresne," he said, gesturing to her as he spoke. "She's just moved here from Seattle and was recommended to us by her former middle school advisor, who said she was one of the best reporters and editors he had."

Kaiah blushed slightly at the compliment, and one of the

older girls at their table leaned over and squeezed her arm while giving her a smile. That made Kaiah blush even more, though she also seemed proud of what Dr. Delmar had said about her.

"There should be a third freshman, as well," Dr. Delmar said. "Where is Noélle Luciér?"

At that moment a short girl entered the room. Chet himself was tall for a freshman, so most girls were shorter than him, but this girl was easily the shortest girl in the freshman class. The way she bounced into the room, however, made her seem larger than life. That was the impression Chet had, anyway … she bounced. She had a round and pretty face with a button nose and rosebud lips and pink-tinged hair done up in short-cropped pigtails, almost like Harley Quinn from the DC comics. And when she walked, she bounced, as if the soles of her shoes were miniature trampolines.

"I'm here!" she said cheerily, giving Dr. Delmar a big smile. "Sorry I'm late. I got caught in a conversation with the art teacher, Mrs. Jennings. Did you know Principal Miller is planning on replacing Charlie the Chicken hawk with a real live chicken?"

Dr. Delmar blinked, then frowned slightly at her.

"How could you possibly know that?" he asked with exasperation.

"When it comes to fashion, Dr. Delmar, I know all about it," Noélle said matter-of-factly. "Not that you could call the mascot costume fashionable. But I did some asking around and found out that Principal Miller doesn't want to have someone else perform as Charlie the Chicken hawk while Gavin Brigantz is missing. He thinks it would be disrespectful to his family. Mrs. Jennings – who has been a friend of my mom's for years – told me she'd talked to one of the science teachers earlier today about not having a mascot at the Homecoming game in two weeks, and he told her that Principal Miller was planning on bringing in a live chicken. Not a lame chicken or anything. A rooster that apparently will run across the field before the game starts."

"Well … I … er …" Dr. Delmar seemed taken aback, and Chet couldn't blame him. This freshman girl having such a nonchalant attitude about carefree conversations with teachers seemed a little far-fetched. But she seemed like the kind of girl who was unaware of how her mannerisms might come across to others, and she just smiled innocently at the older man as he tried to collect himself. Dr. Delmar eventually recovered and waved Noélle over to the empty seat at Chet and Kaiah's pod.

"Please don't be late again, Miss Luciér," Dr. Delmar said. "Even if you are getting scoops for the newspaper."

"Yes sir," Noélle said, plopping into the seat beside Kaiah and giving the adviser a mock salute. Then she looked at Chet and winked. He really didn't know what to think of this girl. She was such an odd combination of confidence and quirkiness.

Dr. Delmar frowned slightly and then collected himself before continuing.

"As most of you know, this year's editor is Sam Chapin," Dr. Delmar said, pointing a hand toward Sam, who was rubbing his nose vigorously as if it itched. "His managing editor will be Elizabeth Cho."

Elizabeth gave a tight-lipped polite smile to everyone in the class … except Chet, at whom she noticeably frowned. Even when she did smile at the others in the room, it was a smile that paled in comparison to the joy-filled one Kaiah had given him earlier.

"For you new people, suffice to say that Sam and Liz are basically in charge," Dr. Delmar said, looking directly at Chet, Kaiah, and Noélle when he said it. "I'm just here to guide and grade."

He chuckled at the alliterative "joke" he'd made before continuing.

"We'll have pitch meetings every Monday, and Sam will help us determine which stories we're going to run each week," Dr. Delmar said. "Liz, as the managing editor, will make sure everyone is meeting deadlines and will essentially manage the flow of stories and art and all of the pieces of the puzzle. She can show you how to file your stories, how the editing process works, and who to work with to get the right photos or designs to go with your stories."

Elizabeth was now looking at the three of them sternly,

no sign of her earlier smile anywhere on her face.

"Do NOT miss deadlines," she said to Chet, Kaiah, and Noélle with no hint of amusement in her voice. "I HATE when people miss deadlines."

Chet and Kaiah nodded emphatically in response. Noélle just blinked her eyes at Liz and then slowly and dramatically returned her gaze to Dr. Delmar, who was smiling at the three of them sympathetically.

"Yes, well, a good portion of your grade in this class is determined by whether or not you can meet deadlines," he said. "But it's also determined by how well you develop your reporter skills. Most of you will be assigned certain beats to cover – from sports to fashion to entertainment … you get the idea. Chet, Kaiah, Miss Luciér … Sam will give you your assignments here in a minute. Usually our freshmen get their feet wet by picking up whatever side stories the editor wants to give them … though it occurs to me that Chet has basically thrown that idea out the window!"

Dr. Delmar paused dramatically to smile at Chet and nod at him in acknowledgment of his accomplishment with the Brigantz story.

"I daresay you've set the bar high for yourself," Dr. Delmar said to him. "We'll see what Sam thinks about letting you pursue the Brigantz story as it continues to develop."

Chet looked at Sam and flinched at the daggers being shot his way. It seemed unlikely that Sam would be amenable to letting Chet continue to pursue such a big story for the paper, but maybe with the success he'd had with the first story it would look bad if Sam tried to pull him off it.

"If you do well with these first assignments – like Mr. Sayer has – you're more likely to be handed bigger assignments going forward," Dr. Delmar continued. "I'll work with you on your stories during one class period every week so that we can develop your skills as writers. That means you need to finish your first drafts earlier than anyone else in the class – preferably by Wednesday. But basically, if you can prove you're willing to work hard and that you're dependable – and that you can report the news that our readers want – then you'll fit right in!"

Chet couldn't help but get more and more excited as Dr. Delmar talked, and his excitement was enough to help him ignore the skeptical look that Sam was directing his way at the moment.

"Please don't get into the habit of contacting me on a Sunday evening, however," Dr. Delmar said with a chuckle, looking at Chet meaningfully as he said it. "Anyway, I think that's about enough of an intro. Sam, do you want to lead us in our first pitch meeting?"

"Yes, Dr. Delmar," Sam said, immediately popping up from his seat and standing at the front of the class. "As we were talking about just a minute ago, the main storyline for this semester is going to be the football team – especially now that our team mascot has gone missing."

He paused long enough to shoot Chet yet another disparaging look before pressing on.

"We have a real shot at making it to the state championship this year, and a lot of people are going to want the inside scoop on the team and everything that goes around it," he said. "That means stories on the coaches and the players and the opponents and anything else you can think of that would interest people about the football team."

Chet's heart sank at Sam's words. Though the senior editor couldn't ignore the story of a missing student, it seemed like his next-best plan to mitigate Chet's flash of popularity was to bury the novelty of the Brigantz story with a mountain of other stories that would be more exciting to the fellow students – specifically stories about the football team. Chet had very little interest in high school football. When it came to sports, he preferred soccer, and that was merely a passing hobby. More importantly, he had no interest in being a sports reporter. It was an extension of entertainment, in his mind, and as such wasn't nearly as important as the meatier news that required good investigative journalism. If Sam was going to make him cover football all semester, then the class he'd been most looking forward to might turn out to be less interesting than he'd hoped. He had to figure out a way to get into Sam's good graces and allow him to continue reporting on Gavin Brigantz.

"Jim and Caleb will lead sports coverage for us," Sam said. "But I'd love to hear any ideas you guys have."

There was a momentary silence before one of the older girls sitting at Chet's pod spoke up. She was an attractive girl who wore a lot of makeup and had her brunette hair in a ponytail.

"The cheer leading team went to a special camp this summer for the first time," the girl said. "I think it would be interesting to do a story about why they went to the camp and how it's going to make them better this year."

"It can't make them any worse," snickered one of the boys at another pod, and half the class laughed with him. Chet assumed that meant the CHS cheer leading squad wasn't very good.

"Not a bad idea, Kim," Sam said. "Go with that. Who else?"

"Oooh! I heard the cheer leading squad was getting new uniforms this year, too," Noélle blurted out. "I'll do an exposé on that for the first issue."

"Excuse me?" Sam said, incredulous. "I hand out the assignments here, thank you very much."

"Are the uniforms hotter?" Caleb asked before Noélle could say anything. He was looking at Noélle with wide eyes, and he seemed oblivious to the fact that every girl in the room was glaring at him.

"Hotter?" Noélle asked, blinking.

"Yeah!" Caleb said. "You know, shorter skirts or thinner tank-tops or something like that?

Chet chuckled to himself at how oblivious Caleb was.

"You're disgusting, Caleb," said Kim, the older girl at Chet's pod who had pitched the original cheerleader story. "Why don't you shut up and let the mature people talk?"

Caleb blinked in surprise and then looked around, finally realizing that the girls in the room were not happy with him. He shrank back and then looked to Sam for help.

"I mean … if they're hotter, it would make for a good story, right Sam?" Caleb said, trying to save face. Sam just shook his head at his friend before turning back to Noélle.

"Fine," he said. "See what you can find out about the new cheer leading uniforms. But I'm not convinced it's an exposé."

"I'll need a photographer," Noélle said, not looking up at Sam while she scribbled a note on a notepad she'd pulled out of her backpack. "And you should probably plan on running some kind of graphic or something of the uniforms. I'll get you art for that."

"Hey! Who's the editor here?" Sam said.

Noélle looked up at Sam and blinked again. Chet guessed she probably did that a lot. She seemed genuinely surprised that people might not find her charming. And to her credit, Sam did seem to soften a bit when he saw the look on her face.

"Yeah … OK," he said, backing down. "A photo of the cheer leading squad is probably a good idea, especially if they have new uniforms. I'll send David with you when you go to do the interview. Talk to Liz after this and she'll arrange everything."

Noélle nodded and smiled, then turned in her chair and looked at Chet with a triumphant gleam in her eyes. He couldn't help but smile back. He was impressed with her tenacity and confidence. It seemed like nothing could faze her joy, and her unconcern for what others thought of her was refreshing … and rare for freshmen girls.

For the next 20 minutes the rest of the class threw out story ideas, most of which Sam approved. Occasionally he would ask probing questions or give out suggestions of people to talk to or follow-up questions to ask in interviews, but for the most part he let the student reporters take their own approach to developing their stories. Chet found this fascinating, and wondered if he'd lead the same way when he one day became editor.

"Don't you have any ideas?" Kaiah whispered into his ear, causing him to jump slightly.

"About football?" Chet said, looking at her skeptically out of the side of his eye. "No. I don't care about football."

Kaiah chuckled. "Me either. But surely they aren't going to fill the whole paper with stories about football … or cheer leading uniforms. What about the school board or other extracurriculars like band or drama? What about news having to do with our teachers or the administrators? There's all kinds of other things to report about."

"I agree," Chet whispered back. "But what can we do about it? We're just lowly freshmen. We have to take what they'll give us."

"Says the guy who has already landed the biggest story of the year …" Kaiah said flatly.

Chet lifted the corner of his mouth and shrugged sheepishly. Kaiah stared him in the eyes for a long, drawn-out moment, then got a determined look on her face and sat up straight while turning toward Sam. Then she raised her hand and cleared her throat.

"Um … Sam," Kaiah said, drawing all eyes to her. "I have an idea."

"Yeah … uh … what's your name?" Sam asked.

"I'm Kaiah," she said with a distinct note of sarcasm in her voice. "This is Chet. That's Noélle."

Chet waved his hand slightly in embarrassment and Sam gave him another frown. Noélle raised her head absently as if only vaguely aware that someone was talking about her. One of the boys in the room snickered again.

"OK, Kaiah," Sam said. "You have an idea?"

"Yes. I noticed that the school parking lot was only half filled when I got here this morning because there's some kind of construction going on or something. This is one of the biggest high schools in the state – 2,600 students, last I heard – and more than 1,000 of them drive to school every day. If they don't have a place to park, what are they supposed to do? And why wasn't the construction finished before school started? What's the timetable for finishing the work? And isn't it a hazard to have an open construction site like that on school grounds? Also, how much did it cost? Did the school board approve only a certain amount and this project ended up going over that, and so they had to halt construction until more money was approved?"

Kaiah's barrage of questions caught Sam off guard, and he blinked a couple of times before replying.

"You're right," he said. "That's a big story and we're definitely covering that. But I'm taking that one. I don't think you're ready for something that big yet. I like your passion, though."

Kaiah's ready smile immediately vanished, and her eyes took on a hint of anger. The skin at the top of her chest and along her throat started to turn a shade of red that Chet would eventually come to recognize as a warning sign that she was furious. But as this was the first time he'd ever been around her, he didn't know that he should do something to head off the explosion that was about to happen.

"Not ready yet?!" Kaiah practically yelled. "Not READY yet?! How could you possibly know that? You don't know anything about me! Maybe Chet and Noélle and I are the best reporters you've ever met! Did you ever think about that?! I mean, Chet has already written what's probably going to be the biggest story of the year!"

"Hey …" Chet whispered under his breath. "Don't bring me into this."

"We ARE ready, thank you very much!" she said, pressing on relentlessly. "And if you don't think so you can go suck an egg!"

Everyone in the class gasped, and Kaiah knew immediately that she'd gone too far. Even Dr. Delmar, who had drifted off into a snooze in the back of the room, had perked up and was now staring at Kaiah. Sam's face was a mixture of anger and disbelief. He obviously was taken aback that a freshman would talk to him like that, and he was trying to decide how angry he should be about it. Then something dawned on him and a slow smile spread across his lips.

"The Gavin story is a big one … too big for one person, actually," Sam said, now turning his wicked smile onto Chet. "So now the two of you can work on it together. I expect to see your first draft by the end of the week. Team up. We'll give you a dual byline. If Liz says your first story is good enough, then I might consider giving you something with a little more meat. But the parking lot story is a steak, and right now you're still babies on the bottle. I'm frankly not convinced that Chet didn't just get lucky this weekend, but I guess we'll see, won't we. If you don't like it, tough. This is my paper and I call the shots. Got it?"

To her credit, Kaiah looked mollified and averted her eyes from Sam's angry gaze. Chet just swallowed and nodded in acquiescence. Sam let his angry glare linger before eventually turning to look at Dr. Delmar.

"I think that about does it," Sam said. "Anything else you need from us Dr. Delmar?"

"No," the old adviser said, frowning to himself as if wondering if he should chastise Sam for the way he'd treated the freshmen. He ultimately decided to let it go. "You all have your assignments. Do your best and let's kick off this year with a great first edition!"

As Chet, Kaiah, and Noélle left The Scribbler newsroom, Noélle couldn't help but laugh at what had just happened.

"That was pretty impressive," she said, smiling at Kaiah. "I mean, your first day and you managed to piss off the editor of the newspaper. Great first impression!"

Kaiah's face colored in embarrassment and she lowered her gaze.

"I suppose it could have been worse," Chet said. "We could have been assigned the crossword puzzle or the comics or something."

Kaiah lifted her head at that and allowed herself a small smile.

"I hate the comics," she said, casting Chet a sidelong glance.

"Ha! Me too!" Chet said. "Such a waste of space!"

"Totally," Kaiah said.

"Did you know they're the most-read part of the news-paper?" A deep voice said from behind them, causing them all to jump. Chet turned around to find Dr. Delmar standing directly behind them.

"What?" Chet asked.

"The comics," Dr. Delmar said. "They're the most-read part of every newspaper. Well, that and the obituaries. People like to laugh and to know who died. Interesting, don't you think?"

"Uh … yeah … I guess," Chet said.

"Don't worry about Sam," Dr. Delmar said, looking at Kaiah. "He'll shake it off. Just do your best on this story and it'll get easier as we go along. OK?"

Kaiah merely nodded her head and kept her eyes on the ground. Dr. Delmar smiled at both of them a moment longer, then turned and walked away down the hall.

"I feel like an idiot," Kaiah said.

"Don't worry about it," Chet said. "I feel like an idiot all the time."

Kaiah turned to him and smiled, and Chet knew things were going to be alright.

"So, you two are a thing, huh?" Noélle asked.

Chet froze, and his face turned so red that it must have resembled a tomato.

"WHAT?!" he squeaked, his voice breaking embarrassingly.

"You're a couple, right?" Noélle pressed. "I mean, I just figured by the way you keep looking at each other and how she included you in everything in class …"

She trailed off with a shrug and looked at the both of them expectantly. It took a long moment for Chet to regather his thoughts, and he did everything in his power to avoid looking at Kaiah.

"Actually, we just met," Chet said. "She moved here from Seattle this summer. Right Kaiah?"

"Uh … yeah," Kaiah said lamely, and Chet finally shot her a look. She had her head down and her hair was covering her face.

"I've lived here my whole life," Chet pressed on, still trying to control his voice and keep it from squeaking again. "Speaking of which, I've never met you before, either. Did you just move here, too?"

"Actually, no," Noélle said, taking the bait and allowing Chet to change the subject – though she smiled slightly at him as if she knew exactly what he was doing. "I've been home-schooled every year before this. Well, every year except first grade when my mom couldn't make up her mind what she wanted to do. But I've wanted to go to a big school like this for years and I finally convinced my mom to let me go this year since it's high school. Now I just have to convince her that it's good for me – you know, get good grades and stuff. But that shouldn't be too hard. None of the classes today seemed too tough."

Chet shrugged and frowned, "I thought math was a little hard."

Kaiah chuckled, which made Chet feel a little better about the awkward moment.

"Math was easy," she said. "Science was the hard one. Besides, it was only day one. It's just gonna get harder from here."

"I don't care about math," he quipped. "I'm gonna be a newspaper editor someday, so all I really care about is English and writing. Math is such a waste of time."

Kaiah chuckled and they stood there in awkward silence for a moment that stretched far too long. Noélle's knowing smile didn't make the moment any better.

"What do you say we go somewhere and start coming up with some ideas about how to do this story?" Kaiah eventually asked, breaking the uncomfortable silence.

"Yeah … OK," Chet said, turning to Noélle and raising an eyebrow as if to say: *Are you gonna join us?*

"You guys go ahead," Noélle said, her knowing smile even wider now. "My mom is picking me up. I'm sure she's already waiting for me outside. I'll see you tomorrow, OK?"

Kaiah and Chet waved to her and then made off for the

school's atrium, where there were more than a dozen tables set up next to the cafeteria. The school also boasted a small café, which was run by the Future Business Leaders of America club.

"I can't stay long," Kaiah said when they arrived at the atrium. "I have to be at band practice in 25 minutes."

"Band practice?" Chet said, somewhat surprised. "You're in band, too?!"

"Yep!"

"What do you play?"

"Triangle!"

Chet looked at Kaiah out of the side of his eye and saw that she was trying to hide a sly grin.

"Ha ha. Very funny."

"No, seriously!" Kaiah insisted. "I'm in the auxiliary – you know, all the xylophones and bells and things like that. And I literally get to play the triangle for one of our songs!"

"That's … awesome … I think?"

"Yeah, it is!" Kaiah said, and then she laughed. "I mean, nobody is ever serious when they say they get to play the triangle. But I really do! It's hilarious!"

Chet joined Kaiah in laughing as they sat down and pulled out notepads from their backpacks. The awkwardness in the hall moments earlier had melted away, and the comfortable familiarity they'd settled into during Newspaper class was quickly returning.

"Well, maybe I'll come to a football game this year just so I can see you play the triangle at halftime or something," Chet said.

"Well yeah you'll come to a football game," Kaiah said seriously. "We're doing a story on the school mascot. You kind of have to go to a game in order to tell the full story."

"Oh … yeah … good point," Chet said.

"So how are we going to tackle this story?" Kaiah asked.

"I have some ideas," Chet said. "Let's put our heads together and plan."

Man Behind the Mascot Shares All

'In the suit you can be whomever you want to be'

By Kim Williams
The Scribbler · Reporter

Some people might not consider it a glamorous job, but Gavin Brigantz thinks performing as Charlie the Chicken hawk is one of the best opportunities he's had as a student at Chetfield High School.

The junior will don the mascot costume for the second year in a row next year, and he said he's looking forward to taking what he learned during this year's escapades and applying it to an exciting senior year.

"When you walk down the halls people know who you are and have a certain expectation for how you'll act or what you'll say," Brigantz said. "But when you're in the suit, you can be whomever you want to be. I love that freedom. I love that I can be as crazy and carefree as I want, and people welcome that. In fact, they expect Charlie the Chicken hawk to be larger-than-life. He's fun and exciting and full of energy, and I love getting to play that role."

Brigantz has been a student of the Chetfield School District since kindergarten when he attended Chetfield Elementary Academy. Over the years he's been known as a bit of a class clown, and many of his friends say they look to him to be the life of the party.

"Gavin is a blast," said Jess Davis, one of Brigantz's classmates. "No matter where you're at – whether it's a party or just hanging out around the house – he's always making people laugh and have fun. And it's not like forced, or anything. He's just fun to be around. It makes perfect sense for him to be Charlie the Chicken hawk."

Despite his popularity, it has been common knowledge that Brigantz has struggled with his grades over the years. Though he has laughed off his poor grades to fellow classmates, school officials have often chastised him for having such a nonchalant attitude toward his overall GPA. In fact, there has been speculation among the student body about whether or not Brigantz would be allowed to continue as Charlie the Chicken hawk next year, as he very nearly ended his junior year with a failing grade in three of his classes. A make-up test in Mr. Boreland's Biology class was enough of a boost to give him a D, which is a passing grade. But Principal Miller said Brigantz will have to show better decision-making next year if he wants to continue to have the privilege of being the school's mascot.

"The school administration does not share students' grades publicly, but I will admit that Mr. Brigantz is on a short leash, for sure," Principal Miller said. "That said, everybody loves what he brings to the table as Charlie the Chicken hawk. His energy and passion at our games and pep rallies really helps to boost morale, and we would all like to see him continue in that endeavor during his senior year."

CHAPTER 3

LORD CHETFIELD ...
THE INVESTIGATIVE REPORTER

het finished reading the previous year's Scribbler article and passed the laptop back to Kaiah. The article was the last of 10 articles about the mascot posted to The Scribbler website over the course of that school year, and Chet was struck with incredulity that the newspaper was giving so much attention to the school mascot.

"Dr. Delmar must really love Charlie the Chicken hawk …" Chet said absently. "I mean, 10 articles about a mascot is kind of excessive."

Kaiah laughed. "Yes, very much."

"Sounds like Gavin is a nice enough guy, though," Chet continued speculatively.

"Really?!" Kaiah snorted. "That's what you got from that

article? C'mon! Clearly he's a clown."

"Hmm … you might be right," Chet said. "So, what should we do? Where do we go from here?"

"Well, we have to talk to someone who knows him," Kaiah said. "We have to try, at least."

"I already have," Chet said. "The Jess girl quoted in the story – I think she's the football team manager – was at practice on Saturday. She basically told me she's Gavin's best friend. I think she has the hots for him, though. But she said she didn't know where he was. Seemed pretty worried about him, actually."

Kaiah just looked at him without saying anything. He could tell she was trying to think of some way to move the story forward, but wasn't coming up with anything. He was drawing blanks, too.

"Nothing in that article says anything about any other extracurriculars he's in," Chet said. "And I don't know the first thing about him. I don't know where he hangs out or who he hangs out with or even what kinds of things he likes to do outside of school. I mean, I don't even know when or where his classes are!"

"Well, that's the first place to start," Kaiah said. "Why don't you go to the office and ask the secretary for Gavin's class schedule?"

"What, by myself?" Chet asked.

"Yes," Kaiah said. "I have to go to band."

"Oh, right … band. But what do I do if they won't give it to me?"

"Be insistent," Kaiah said, smiling at him playfully.

Chet rolled his eyes and then started gathering his things into his backpack as Kaiah stood up and did the same. In the 20 minutes they'd spent together, they'd come up with some key questions they needed answered before they could write the next phase of the story, and they'd come up with a basic timeline on both the missing mascot costume and Gavin's disappearance. Chet was impressed with how Kaiah's brain worked, and he discovered that he really liked working with her.

"So, let's say I get his class schedule," Chet said. "What then?"

"Then we go to every one of his classes and start asking if anyone knows him," Kaiah said. "We can try to get a sense of whether anyone noticed anything unusual about the last few days."

"Oh, right," Chet said. "Makes sense … except, school just started today and Gavin disappeared last week. How is anyone gonna know anything?"

Kaiah favored him with another smile and then started to walk away.

"We'll figure that out tomorrow," she said. "Meet me back here at this table in the morning before first bell."

"OK!" Chet said. "See you tomorrow."

He continued to watch her walk away until she disappeared through a set of double doors that led to the wing that housed the music department. Then he glanced down at his phone and noticed the time. His mother would be waiting for him outside.

He hurried up the stairs and to the office. The secretary behind the front desk turned out to be a student – a senior girl was working as a student assistant in the office.

"Hi," Chet said, smiling and trying to be as friendly as possible. "I'm Chet."

The girl looked at him without smiling and then nodded, waiting for him to tell her what he wanted.

"Right … um … I'm one of the reporters for the school paper and I need the class schedule for Gavin Brigantz please," Chet said all in a rush.

She blinked at him and then frowned slightly.

"You want me to give you another student's schedule?" she asked, voice dripping with sarcasm. "A student who is part of an active police investigation?"

"Well, yeah …" Chet said, trying to remain cheerful and friendly. "What's wrong with that? Not like it's a state secret or anything."

"Sorry," she said, her voice indicating she was anything but sorry. "We don't just give out that kind of information."

"Oh, come on!" Chet said. "I just need to know what classes he's in."

"Why?" she asked.

"Because I need to know how to find him," Chet said, opting for honesty. "I'm hoping someone in one of his classes knows him, or saw him recently, or knows something about what happened."

"Huh … sounds smart, but I can't give you that information," she said, the put-upon frown returning.

"Ugh, seriously?!"

"Yes. Seriously."

"Is there someone else I can ask?"

The senior girl didn't like that question, and her frown turned into an angry scowl.

"No."

Chet sighed. She was obviously a lost cause. He started to turn away, but then noticed Principal Miller walking down the hallway a few feet away from the front desk.

"Mr. Miller!" Chet yelled, startling the girl and making her jump. "Mr. Miller! Can I talk to you about Gavin Brigantz please?!"

Principal Miller stopped and turned toward Chet. He frowned in thought for a moment, then started walking toward the front of the office.

"What's this?" Principal Miller asked.

"Sorry, Mr. Miller," the girl said, interjecting before Chet could answer. "This freshman doesn't know the rules yet. He won't bother you anymore."

"That's alright," Principal Miller said. "What does he want?"

"He wants me to give him another student's class schedule," she said, turning her angry scowl to Chet again.

Principal Miller raised a questioning eyebrow and then turned his gaze on Chet.

"What's your name, young man?"

"Uh … Chet Sayer, sir," Chet answered.

"Nice to meet you, Chet," Principal Miller responded. "You're the one who wrote the article about Gavin, aren't you?"

"Yes sir!" Chet said, trying unsuccessfully not to beam. "I'm following up on that story, actually. I thought maybe if I could get Gavin's class schedule I could start asking some of the people in his classes if they know anything. I know it's a long shot, but I have to start somewhere."

"Ah," Principal Miller said. "I see. Makes sense. Unfortunately, we can't give out that kind of information."

The senior girl smiled in satisfaction and crossed her arms as she looked at Chet in triumph.

"But …" Principal Miller continued, "I can tell you that Gavin liked to hang out with Jess Davis. She'd probably be a good person to talk to.

"Yeah, I met her already," Chet said. "She doesn't know where he is. She said she's been trying to get ahold of him since Friday, but he hasn't answered any of her messages."

"Ah, well … I'm sorry we couldn't be of more help," Principal Miller said, then turned away and headed back down the hall.

Chet left the office quickly before the girl could say anything else, then made his way outside to the pick-up curb, where his mother was waiting. Instead of getting in, however, he waved at her and made a signal with his hand that he wanted her to roll down the window.

"Hi Mom," he said cheerily. "How are you?"

"I'm fine," she said curtly. She was definitely still mad at him. "What's going on?"

"Well, I did so well on my first newspaper assignment that the editor wants me to keep going with the story," he said, smiling brightly as he stretched the truth. "And I need to stay after school to finish it."

"On your first day?" she asked, incredulous.

"Yeah … I have to go to football practice," Chet said, wincing at the thought.

"Football? Again? You were just there on Saturday. Wait, is this about that missing kid?"

"Yes …" Chet said hesitantly, knowing that his mom was

going to immediately start worrying about his safety.

"Chet, you be careful," his mom said seriously. "You don't know what happened to that boy, or what kinds of things he was into. Don't go snooping in places and get yourself in trouble like your father did, just because you're trying to be the hot-shot new reporter for the school paper."

"OK, Mom," Chet said, trying hard not to roll his eyes at her. Why did she always have to be so dramatic? "Anyway, sorry for the short notice. I think maybe I can get a ride with Chunk after practice or something."

"OK ..." she said after a long pause. "I'm serious, young man. You don't do anything stupid just trying to get a story. It's not worth it."

"OK, Mom," Chet said again. "I promise."

"Alright ... I'm choosing to trust you," she said, shaking her head as if trying to rid her mind of the flurry of worries that had suddenly popped up. "Please don't let me down again. I'll see you at home for dinner."

"Thanks, Mom! Love you!"

Chet immediately turned away and started walking toward the football field. He could hear his mom drive away behind him. He wasn't sure what he expected to discover at football practice, but he felt an itch to keep digging with Jess and he knew he'd never be able to sit still at home without having some of his questions answered.

When he arrived at the football field, the players were

just finishing with one of their drills and were jogging to the sideline to get drinks. Chunk saw Chet walking up and veered away from his teammates, running up to his friend with a big grin on his face.

"Two football practices in a row!" the big lineman said. "I'm gonna start thinking you're an actual football fan now!"

Chet winced and then rolled his eyes at his friend. "Ha ha," he said humorlessly. "You know I'm here to follow up on the Gavin story."

"Oh yes," Chunk said. "You're very popular now. Lord Chetfield the investigative reporter."

Chet let out a groan. But instead of rising to his friend's bait he just ignored him.

"I'll need a ride home tonight, if that's alright," Chet said, looking around on the sideline for some sign of Jess, the team manager. Chunk just nodded and turned to see what Chet was looking at. The senior girl didn't seem to be anywhere on the field, and two other students – one a boy and one a girl – were handing out drinks to the players and squeezing water or Gatorade into their mouths from sports bottles. Chet frowned, curious as to why Jess wasn't there.

"Any idea where Jess is?" he asked Chunk without looking at him.

"Nope," Chunk said simply. Chet shot him a sidelong glance and then continued his perusal of the football team.

"Think Kevin and Steve would talk to me about Gavin

anymore?" Chet pressed.

"Uh … maybe," Chunk said noncommittally. "I wouldn't try to talk to them now, though. Coach only gave us a five-minute break."

Chet nodded and then became distracted by a noise he heard in the distance. It sounded like drums of some sort, and when he looked across the field, he saw that the school's marching band was rehearsing on the junior varsity field that sat on a slight rise above the main building. Chetfield High School was a big enough school that it had a varsity and a JV team for just about every sport, and in addition to the football fields the school also boasted a soccer field, a baseball diamond, and a large open field where the girl's lacrosse team practiced and played. Just beyond that field was a small copse of woods that surrounded the old water plant, which had long been abandoned and was overgrown with vegetation and covered copiously with graffiti.

The drums coming from the marching band were soon joined by brass instruments, and Chet considered walking over there to see if he could catch a glimpse of Kaiah playing triangle. He chuckled at the mental image of that. Chunk helped him make his decision when a moment later he clapped his friend on the shoulder and made his way back onto the football field to continue practice. Chet slowly began walking around the football field and up the hill to the JV field where the band was playing.

CHS was a school that boasted nearly 2,600 students,

which meant it was one of the larger high schools in the state. As such, it had a rather large marching band, and as Chet came up over the rise he saw nearly 200 students making odd-shaped formations on the field while playing their various instruments. Chet winced at some of the bad notes that were being played as the students marched.

He immediately spotted Kaiah, who was with the auxiliary group at the extreme edge of the field, just in front of the small stand of bleachers. There were xylophones and timpani drums and wind chimes and a variety of other random instruments in the group – including an amplifier with an electric guitar hooked up to it. Kaiah was toward the edge of the group, holding her triangle in one hand and the small metal stick in her other, just slightly above the instrument ready to strike it when it was time to do so. Chet chuckled at the concentration on her face. She was very focused and didn't even notice him walking around the edge of the field to sit on one of the bleachers.

Chet was just starting to recognize the tune the band was playing as a popular musical score to one of the biggest movies of the previous year when the band teacher blew his whistle and shouted to everyone to take a five-minute break before resetting and starting from the top. Kaiah set her triangle on a music stand and looked toward Chet. She smiled widely, and immediately started to make her way toward him.

"So, what did you think?" Kaiah asked, tossing her hair to the side as she nodded to the field and the band behind her.

"You are easily the best triangle player I've ever met," Chet said with mock sincerity. "Seriously. The Boston Pops should hire you immediately. You need to go on a world tour."

Kaiah laughed and smiled deeply, rolling her eyes at the same time. "What are you doing here?" she asked.

"The school office wouldn't give me Gavin's class schedule, so I decided to try to talk to Jess again," Chet said, nodding toward the larger football field where the team was practicing. "But she wasn't there. Then I heard the band, so I thought I'd come ... check it out."

Chet hoped Kaiah hadn't noticed the slight pause at the end of what he said when he'd corrected himself from saying "check you out." He hadn't meant it that way, and honestly hadn't really considered what he was saying until the words had been about to tumble out of his mouth. It was a startling realization in that moment of just how much he liked her. He'd never really considered the idea of a girlfriend before, and the notion was surprising. Kaiah must have noticed a strange look on his face as he contemplated the idea, because her smile vanished and a concerned look replaced it.

"What's wrong?" she asked.

"Nothing!" he replied, too forcefully he realized. "I was just considering what to do next."

"Well, I'm glad you came," she said. "I heard something on the way to band practice that I wanted to tell you."

Chet raised an eyebrow at her.

"We have to roll out all the auxiliary instruments to the field every day, and it always takes longer than the rest of the band," she said. "We have to go around the back half of the school because the cart we use is too wide to fit through anything but the double doors at the front and back of the school … which means we have to wind through the hallway that passes along the science labs."

Chet nodded, trying to mask his impatience as he waited for Kaiah to get to the point. He must not have done a good job of hiding it, however, as she smiled slightly as if she knew exactly what he was thinking.

"The point is, we rolled past the science labs and I over-heard the biology teacher Mr. Boreland talking on his cell phone," she continued, lowering her voice and leaning in conspiratorially. "He seemed really angry. Whoever he was talking to owed him money or something."

"OK …" Chet said, confused as to why she thought this was important. "What has this got to do with anything? He could have been talking to his wife, or a friend, or the bank, or a million other people."

Kaiah frowned at him – obviously she thought this was more important than he did.

"I don't think he was talking to his wife," Kaiah said, exasperated. "I mean, if I was his wife and he was talking to me like that, I'd make him sleep on the sofa for a month!"

Chet chuckled and then shrugged his shoulders.

"Whatever," he said. "My point is that it doesn't have anything to do with Gavin."

"Well, I didn't say that it did ..." Kaiah said, a hurt look coming across her face. "I just thought it was unusual that he would be yelling like that at someone while at school. I mean, he was really yelling loudly, and he told whoever he was yelling at that they only had one more week to pay up."

Chet gave her a long look as she gazed at him expectantly. He didn't know what to say, and just shrugged his shoulders at her. If he was being honest, he thought she was grabbing at anything that sounded even the slightest bit off, in the hopes that it would turn into a big story and she could "catch up" to him in the realm of breaking big stories. He wasn't going to tell her that, though.

A moment later the band teacher blew his whistle, indicating that the five-minute break was over and Kaiah needed to return to her station. She frowned at him again and then turned to walk away.

"Just forget it," she said over her shoulder. "I'm just jumpy, I guess ... looking for anything out of the ordinary for a clue. You're probably right about Mr. Boreland. Sorry I brought it up."

Though she tried to hide it, Chet saw the hurt look on her face. He didn't know what to say, though, and just sat there staring at her back. What did she expect him to do, march into Mr. Boreland's office and confront him about a phone call another student had overheard while passing in the hallway?! Chet couldn't even imagine the thought of it. The very notion made him want to run the other way. Not only would it be disrespectful, but he could get into trouble. Besides, he hated confrontation. He'd get into an argument with someone if something didn't make sense, or if they were doing something obviously wrong, but he avoided unnecessary conflict as often as he possibly could. The idea of purposefully creating conflict with an adult – a teacher – just in the hopes of getting a scrap of a clue for a story was something he would never even think about.

Annoyed at the idea, Chet popped off the bleacher and started walking away from the practice field. Instead of going back the way he'd come, he decided to walk around behind the school and head toward the rear entrance, which Kaiah had just mentioned a moment before. He wasn't sure what made him go that way other than the conversation he'd just had made him realize he'd never been to that part of the school before and he was curious. He also needed to think, and the random idea of walking around the entire school seemed an intriguing notion at the moment.

He was nearly to the school's back entrance – a large, double-door exit through which Kaiah's band mates could easily push a cart – when he noticed a commotion off to his left by the baseball field. A group of boys were setting something up on the pitcher's mound, and as Chet squinted to get a better look he realized it was the Charlie the Chicken hawk costume, set up on a pole like a scarecrow.

Without thinking, Chet immediately raced toward the field. As he drew closer he saw a couple of the boys get out spray paint cans and start painting the costume blue. CHS's colors were red and silver, but their rival school Pickering boasted blue and gold colors. It was obvious that these boys were from that school and were defaming the stolen mascot costume. Another boy was using a blue spray paint can to write something onto the field; Chet saw that it said: "CHS CHICKEN-SUCKS!"

"Hey!" Chet yelled as he ran onto the baseball field, rapidly approaching the group of boys. "Hey, where did you get that costume?!"

The boys looked up in surprise, obviously not expecting to be found so quickly. Two of them jumped and started to run away, but then they looked over Chet's shoulder and noticed he was alone. The tension eased out of their bodies and instead of bolting, they stood up a little straighter and adopted sneers. There were five of them, and now that Chet was close to them he could see they were all big. Obviously, they were football players.

"Well … well … well," one of the boys said with a wide grin. "What do we have here? Looks like a little freshman prick has come to save the day, eh?"

The other boys laughed, and with a signal from the leader two of them rushed Chet and grabbed his arms before he could even think to run away. They handled him roughly, but it didn't hurt too much. Chet swallowed the lump in his throat and tried to think of what to say.

"Where did you get that costume?" he asked again, though with far less conviction in his voice this time.

The boys laughed, and the ring-leader – a swarthy, stocky kid with a pudgy nose and big, meaty hands – crossed his arms while slowly assessing Chet. He had big arms and crossing them only accentuated his muscles. There was a dangerous look in his eyes that Chet didn't like.

"We found it," the older boy finally answered, shrugging his shoulders. "What're you gonna do about it?"

"Where'd you find it?" Chet pressed. The older boy scowled at him in return.

"None of your business where we found it," he said, taking a couple of threatening steps forward so that his face was right in front of Chet's.

"You know you're gonna get in major trouble for this, right?" Chet said, unable to keep the tremor from his voice but somehow finding the courage to be defiant. The ring-leader threw his head back and let out a loud laugh. The others followed suit, and the ones with the paint cans smiled as they went back to their work.

"C'mon Dave, let him have it," said one of the boys holding Chet's arms. "Little punk deserves it."

Dave – the ring-leader – looked at his friend and then back down to Chet.

"Why would we get in trouble?" the boy sneered. "Who's gonna tell anyone we were here? Not you … right?"

"Of course I am!" Chet replied without thinking, then winced as he realized what he'd said. "I mean … no, I won't tell anybody … if you tell me where you found the costume."

Dave scowled at Chet again and squeezed his hands tight into fists.

"Why do you care so much about it?" the boy holding his arm asked with a sneer. "You got a thing for chickens?"

"Haha! Yeah!" the other boy holding his arm said. "Chicken Boy loves his chickens! If you loved it so much you shouldn't have thrown it away!"

"Shut up, Jimmy," Dave said, turning his scowl to the boy who had just talked.

"What?!" Jimmy asked defensively. "They threw it away like it was trash! What difference does it make if Chicken Boy knows we found it with some other junk by that old building?"

"I said shut up, Jimmy!" Dave replied, his scowl deepening.

"What old building?" Chet interjected, unwisely pressing the issue.

Dave didn't even hesitate in taking a swing and clocking him in the eye. The pain was immediate – like a hammer had just smashed into the side of his face. Everything went black for a minute, and then Chet's eyes flashed little spar-kling lights as he tried to focus through the tears that were forming. He realized he was now lying on the ground, and he shook his head to clear the cobwebs. Dave kicked up a big cloud of dust right into Chet's face, and Chet immediately started hacking and wiping the grit out of his eyes. The other two boys were laughing behind his back.

A moment later Chet heard something behind him in the distance, and when he'd gotten enough of the dirt out of his eyes to see again, he noticed that Dave and the other boys were looking over his shoulders at something. The arrogant looks were no longer on their faces. Now they looked star-tled and more than a little bit concerned.

"C'mon!" Dave yelled to the others. "Let's get out of here."

The other boys nodded and the five of them immediately made off. They'd accomplished what they'd wanted to accom-plish, though. Charlie the Chicken hawk was displayed as a scarecrow right in the middle of the baseball diamond. He was painted blue from head to toe, with just a hint of his red costume peeking out in places. The words scrawled on the field were offensive. Chet just shook his head and continued to wipe the dirt out of his eyes, spitting now and then to get rid of the grit that had become mud in his mouth.

A moment later Chunk and a few of the other football players ran up to him. That was what Dave and the other boys had seen in the distance. Chunk reached down and helped Chet to his feet.

"You OK?" Chunk asked. Chet just nodded and spat again. "What were you thinking? Did you really think you could take on five guys by yourself?"

Chet blushed and lowered his head in embarrassment, but not before he caught a look from Kevin and Steve out of the corner of his eye. Those looks seemed filled with respect – as if they were impressed that a skinny freshman like Chet would try to take on five muscled-up football players in defense of the school's honor.

"I didn't think, honestly," Chet said. "I just saw them and started running. Stupid ..."

Chunk snorted and Kevin and Steve chuckled. A few other football players had continued chasing the five offenders into the woods, but now they were making their way back, obviously giving up on the chase. They stood on the field and looked down at the words on the ground. Angry scowls covered their faces. Chet looked at his friend and saw the same look of anger there, as well.

"Well, at least you found the Chicken hawk costume, right?" Chunk said flatly.

"They said they found it with some other junk," Chet said, reaching up and touching his face gingerly. "I dunno where. They said it was by some old building."

Chunk just shrugged as he examined the scarecrow mascot in front of them. The other boys were starting to comment on the things they'd do to Pickering to get revenge, and the ideas were quickly becoming more and more severe.

"Your eye is gonna be five shades of black in the morning," Chunk said suddenly, letting out a chuckle. "It's already starting to turn purple."

Chet reached a hand to his eye again and winced in pain.

"You're also gonna be the most popular kid in school, I bet," Chuck continued. "First you write the story about Gavin going missing, then you try to take on five rival football players all by yourself! If I didn't know you better, I'd think you were trying to make a name for yourself, dude."

Chet blinked in surprise and then frowned at his friend. Chunk just laughed again and then walked over to the other football players and joined in the conversation. Some of the ideas they were coming up with for retaliation were truly diabolical, and Chet just shook his head.

Noticing the boys with their angry scowls staring at the disfigured chicken hawk costume, Chet realized it was the perfect picture for the newspaper. He quickly pulled out his phone and snapped a few pictures. None of the boys seemed to care, so he took as many as he could to make sure he had lots of options to show Sam and Liz.

Chetfield City Water Plant: A History

When Chetfield was founded in 1817 by Edward Chetfield – one of the descendants of Lord Robert Chetfield of Wales – it was nothing more than a few log houses and one sawmill on the edge of Licking River. Chetfield was known throughout the world as one of the premier authorities on microbiology, especially water micro-organisms. He studied water purification and was an apprentice of Robert Thom, who built the first municipal water treatment plant in 1804 in Scotland. It was Chetfield's dream to build a new and improved water treatment plant in America.

Chetfield was ahead of his time when he developed the slow sand filter, which consisted of a two-foot layer of sand with layers of shells, gravel and bricks beneath. He spent much of his inherited fortune building the filter and transporting all of the necessary materials from England to America – much to his family's chagrin. Though a novelty that brought the town notoriety on a global scale, the filter wasn't something that could accommodate a large population, and as such it wasn't widely used, despite the fact that it was capable of clearing 95 percent of impurities from the water.

Chetfield never accomplished his bigger dream of giving the entire town filtered municipal water, and his fortune ran out, leaving his family destitute. What he did accomplish, however, was a legacy of cutting-edge water filtration technology that the Chetfield City Water Plant continues to uphold to this day.

The original water works were constructed by the Lumbarger Company Limited in 1897, and in 1913 the city of Chetfield – which by that time boasted a population of 17,000, with seven churches, five grocery stores, two flour mills, and the beginnings of electricity in homes and businesses – acquired the system. Drop wells were constructed and fitted with an air lift system. A dam was soon built to manufacture a man-made lake to serve as the source of the city's primary water. The water treatment works was constructed adjacent to this lake in 1917.

Taking a cue from Edward Chetfield, the city chose to employ the services of an architect who was ahead of his time – Alsbet Samuelsson. Hailing from Sweden, this young architect designed a waterworks that would incorporate a labyrinthine style that featured many halls and rooms that became known throughout the region as the "water maze." Employees of the water works have shared stories of getting lost in the halls of the water maze many times over the years. Though it became an endearing quality of the facility, it also was one of the features that led the company to shut it down and build a newer, more updated facility in 1982.

Completed in 1984, the Chetfield City Water Plant is a state-of-the-art municipal water filtration and distribution center that provides clean water for the city and its surrounding rural neighbors. The original water plant, however, still stands and has become a local legend for its tales of haunted halls and ghost stories of children getting lost in the water maze.

CHAPTER 4
SAY HELLO TO THE NEWS HAWKs

A wide yawn cracked Chet's jaw as he finished reading from the pamphlet that had been handed out to his Social Studies class. He winced and tried yet again to discipline himself from touching his eye. Chunk had been right about the black eye – when Chet had looked at himself in the mirror that morning it was black and purple and swollen almost halfway shut. His mother had not been happy when he'd sat at the table for breakfast, though his little sister, Chloe, had thought it to be the funniest thing she'd seen in a while and wouldn't stop laughing.

Social Studies was a two-hour class that he only had to take on Tuesdays and Thursdays, and it doubled as a study hall. The good part of the class was that it alternated with Physical Education, which meant he only had to take that class on Mondays, Wednesdays and Fridays. The bad part of the class was that it was boring. But as long as he could tolerate the hour's worth of lecture that came at the beginning of the two-hour period, the remainder of the class was open to do whatever he wanted. And the best part was that it happened to be one of the classes he shared with Chunk. Coincidentally, both Kaiah and Noélle were also in the class.

The old water plant that his class was currently hearing about from the monotonous Mrs. Whisman sat adjacent to the school, and through the classroom window he could see the tops of the building peeking out from among the trees on the other side of the baseball field. It was one of more than a dozen buildings in town designed by Alsbet Samuelsson, who was the grandfather of the architect his father had been investigating. It was Samuelson's designs that had inspired his grandson to become an architect himself, and many of the treasure seekers around the world speculated that there were clues to the supposed treasure hiding in some of the elder Samuelson's old buildings. Chet had often wondered if the old water plant held any clues to his father's untimely death. Now, staring out the window listening to Mrs. Whisman drone on and on, he tried not to think about it too much. Even so, he couldn't help wondering it that building was where the Pickering boys had found the discarded Charlie costume – if they'd even been telling the truth in the first place. Despite what they'd done to him, Chet was inclined to believe they'd been telling the truth.

"The original water plant is a valuable piece of our town's history," Mrs. Whisman said. "I'd love to be able to take you on a tour this semester, but unfortunately the plant has been slated for demolition and the city has forbidden access to the facility while they begin the demolition process."

"What?!" Chet exclaimed, sitting up in his seat and frowning at the teacher. "They're destroying the water plant?"

"Yes …" Mrs. Whisman replied, clearly confused as to why Chet was so distraught. "They've told us to make sure none of you try to do anything stupid, like sneak onto the grounds at night. Eventually they'll use explosives to bring the building down, and you'll all be invited to view it from a safe distance when they do."

"Explosives?!" Chunk exclaimed loudly. "Cool!"

"Not cool, Mr. Edwards," Mrs. Whisman replied immediately with a scowl. "It's not like fireworks, and there won't be a big fireball when it explodes. It's building demolition explosives, which makes the building implode and collapse upon itself. Rather underwhelming, actually – but dangerous if you're caught inside, as the massive concrete structure would crush you. Not the best way to go. So, don't get any ideas about trying to sneak in because you'd likely get lost in the water maze and get stuck in there at the wrong time."

Mrs. Whisman's stern look lingered on Chunk, who gave a sheepish smile and nodded in acquiescence. When she looked away, Chet leaned over to his friend and whispered fiercely.

"We have to go explore that water maze!" Chet hissed as Mrs. Whisman continued to share about the history of the water plant and its impact on the evolution of the town. "I'm almost certain that's where the Pickering boys found the Charlie costume, plus it's one of the buildings my dad was investigating. Maybe there's a clue there about how he died."

Chunk shrugged uncomfortably as he looked at his friend. Chet looked around to see if anyone else had heard what he'd whispered and noticed that Kaiah was giving him a sidelong frown – a kind of chastising look that he was quickly becoming used to. She did it whenever she thought he was being ridiculous, which seemed to be often. When she'd seen his eye that morning, she'd frowned at him so harshly that he'd felt deeply ashamed. Obviously, she had no respect for boys who got in fights. In fact, she'd said as much nearly half a dozen times already that day.

"Yeah, sure … if you want to get trapped in a haunted maze," Chunk whispered back fiercely.

Cheat turned back to his friend and grinned. "Sounds like fun!"

Chunk frowned and Chet snickered. For someone so large and muscular, Chunk really was kind of a baby when it came to scary things. He never liked to go with Chet to haunted houses or corn mazes around Halloween, and he downright refused to watch any scary movies.

"Don't even think about it," Kaiah whispered, leaning toward the two of them. "You heard Mrs. Whisman – you could get hurt!"

Chet frowned as he lowered his head and looked out the window again at the old water plant's sun-bleached walls. Vagrants had painted symbols and various street art onto the walls, and with the overgrowth of vegetation around the building it looked like an uninviting place. Chet imagined what it might be like to visit the place at night. He realized he had no desire to get lost in that maze of halls during the day, let alone at night. But if there was even the slightest chance of a clue to what had happened to his dad, he had to take a chance. Before he could think much more on it, Mrs. Whisman released them to the study hall portion of their time, which meant they were free to talk. Noélle started the conversation with a bombshell.

"Hey, did you guys hear that Gavin Brigantz's mom is missing now?" she said conspiratorially.

"Really?!" Chet replied, scooting around in his chair to face her. Kaiah did the same. Chet noticed that Chunk, who was sitting on the other side of him, was also intrigued and leaning in to listen to Noélle. The short-statured girl blinked at Chet as she stared at his black eye, and she winced before quickly looking away from his face and glancing at Kaiah, instead.

"Mrs. Jennings said something about it to my mom when she dropped me off this morning," she said confidently. "They're friends, you know."

"Yeah, you told us that yesterday in newspaper class," Kaiah said impatiently. "What else did she say?"

"She said the new cheerleader uniforms arrived yesterday and the team is going to be doing a full practice in them after school today," Noélle replied.

"Really?!" Chunk said eagerly, his eyes big. Chet gave him a withering look. "What? Don't tell me you don't want to see that."

Chet started to reply, then snuck a look at Kaiah and Noélle. Both of them were frowning at him. He shook his head at Chunk and tried to give him a signal with his eyes to drop it.

"I don't care about cheerleader uniforms," Kaiah said to Noélle after another glare at Chet. "I meant, what else did she say about Gavin's mom?"

"Oh … nothing really," Noélle said with a shrug. "Just that the police went by her house last night to check in and she wasn't there. Apparently, they waited around all night and she never came home. Some guy knocked on her door around 10 p.m., but other than that nothing happened at her house the entire night. Mrs. Jennings thinks it's nothing unusual, though. Apparently both Gavin's parents are heavy drinkers, and Mrs. Jennings thinks she probably got drunk and passed out somewhere."

"That's sad," Kaiah said, and everyone else looked at her in silence as they digested Noélle's words. Chet wondered whether or not he agreed with Mrs. Jenning's assessment of the situation. Ultimately, he decided he didn't have enough information to make any kind of decision.

"Oh, I forgot," Noélle said suddenly, drawing back everyone's attention. "She also said the police were going to start questioning some of the other senior boys today. Apparently, there's a rumor that Gavin owed some of the other seniors some money or something. Mrs. Jennings was kind of vague about that part."

Chet and Kaiah shared a startled look.

"What's that look?" Chunk asked quickly.

Chet started to answer, then looked at Kaiah and nodded to her to proceed.

"I overheard Mr. Boreland yelling on the phone yesterday about someone owing him money," Kaiah answered. "Chet didn't think it had anything to do with anything, though."

She shot him an accusing look, and Chet scowled back at her.

"I still don't," he said. "One thing probably doesn't have anything to do with the other."

"Well, it is kind of weird, don't you think?" Kaiah pressed. "I mean, Gavin owes money to some other boys and then goes missing, and now someone owes money to Mr. Boreland. That's a little coincidental, don't you think?"

Chet shrugged and looked at Chunk, who had a thoughtful look on his face.

"It probably has more to do with the poker game," Chunk said, and Chet nodded in agreement.

"What's this?" Kaiah asked. "What poker game?"

Chet shot her a triumphant grin, proud of himself for having the one-up on her.

"A couple of the seniors on the football team invited me and Chunk to a poker game this Friday," Chet explained quickly. "They said something about how Gavin had won a hundred dollars last time he played."

Kaiah's eyes got big.

"You think something happened to him because he was gambling?" she asked.

"Poker isn't gambling," Chunk replied immediately. "Everybody says that, but it's really more a game of skill. Not much different than football, really."

"Yeah … except you don't have to get tackled by a 200-pound Chicken hawk when you're playing cards," Noélle quipped.

Chunk grinned at her. "True," he said with a chuckle.

"Whatever," Kaiah said. "If he won a hundred dollars, that means somebody else lost that much money. Surely they weren't happy about that."

"Yeah … I dunno," Chet said, thinking through this new information. "I doubt anyone would do anything bad to Gavin just because of a poker game. That seems like a stretch. And it's even more of a stretch that Mr. Boreland would be involved."

"Well you guys have to find out what happened," Kaiah said without hesitation. "Talk to those guys on the football team. Get the scoop."

"We can talk to them at the poker game on Friday," Chet said, and Chunk nodded.

"That's three days from now!" Kaiah said. "We can't wait for that!"

Chet just blinked at her, not knowing what to say in response.

"Sorry," Kaiah said, realizing she'd become more passionate than she'd intended to be. "I just mean, we have to file our first draft of the story tomorrow, remember. Dr. Delmar said he wants freshmen to file their stories by Wednesday."

"Ugh ... yeah, I forgot," Chet said. "Maybe Sam will let us off the hook if I give him the story about my fight with the Pickering boys."

Kaiah snorted and Noélle gave him an appraising look.

"What?" Chet said defensively. "I got a great picture to go with it. Besides, everyone will want to read about that."

Chunk laughed and Kaiah shot daggers at him with her eyes, which just made him laugh even more.

"You know, I think Aaron Johnson goes to that poker game, too," Noélle said suddenly, as if she'd just remembered something.

"Who?" Kaiah and Chet replied simultaneously.

"Our quarterback," Chunk answered for her. "How do you know he plays in that game, though?"

"His girlfriend is the cheer captain. I heard her talking to one of the other girls yesterday about being mad that Aaron wanted to hang out with his 'poker buddies' instead of her last Friday night," Noélle used air quotes with her fingers when she talked, and she began to nod her head as she considered what she'd overheard the day before. "I didn't think much about it at the time. Girls like her are always complaining about their boyfriends. But obviously it means that he goes to the same poker game. Maybe he knows something."

"Or maybe his girlfriend does ..." Kaiah said quietly, staring off into space as she considered what Noélle had said. "You should talk to her."

"OK ... but that means I get to be on your byline," Noélle said.

Chet rolled his eyes, which made his black eye hurt. Kaiah noticed when he winced and allowed herself a small, satisfied smile, which irritated Chet.

"Of course," Kaiah said to Noélle. "You're one of the News Hawks, too, after all!"

"News Hawks?" Chet asked, confused. Noélle also seemed to have no idea what Kaiah was talking about. Kaiah blushed slightly but tried to cover it up by straightening in her seat and looking them boldly in the eyes.

"Yeah, News Hawks!" she said confidently. "That's the

name I use for us in my head … I mean, the three of us freshmen on the newspaper team, that is."

Chet and Noélle blinked, not knowing what to say. Into that awkward silence, Chunk cleared his throat loudly.

"Um … excuse me … but there are four of us, thank you very much," he said with a straight face, no hint of a smile on his lips, though his eyes did dance with mirth.

"Uh … OK … the four of us, I guess," Kaiah said, not sure what to make of Chunk's forced entrance into their little cohort.

"News Hawks …" Noélle said as if tasting the name on her lips for the first time. "I kind of like it."

Chet nodded emphatically and smiled. "Me too!" he said, looking at Kaiah. She smiled in return – a genuine smile this time – and blushed a little more at the attention she'd drawn upon herself.

"So, Chet and Chunk are gonna interview the football guys at the poker game, and Noélle is gonna talk to the cheer captain," Kaiah said. "What am I gonna do?"

"You're gonna find Gavin's mom," Chet said immediately. "Or someone from his family, at least."

"What?!" Kaiah said, sitting up straight again and looking at him with a hint of panic in her eyes.

"You know we have to," Chet said. "We can't write this story without at least trying to get some information from his family. You're the perfect person to do it. We can't tell this story without the family angle."

Kaiah's face turned pale and she looked like she wasn't feeling well, but she slowly nodded her head in agreement. Noélle gave her a consoling pat on the shoulder and then turned to look back at Chet.

"What else, Chief?" she asked, smiling at the playful moniker. He couldn't help but smile in return. It was the kind of nickname that many editors around the world were given by a newspaper staff for whom they were fond.

"I think that should just about cover it," he said. "We'll compare notes tomorrow at lunch."

The other three nodded their heads before easing back into their seats and turning their attention to the worksheets Mrs. Whisman had given them. Chet smiled as he heard Chunk whispering "News Hawks" over and over to himself as he worked.

It is a good name, Chet thought.

Pickering High Principal Offers Official Apology Following Chicken Hawk Prank

By Jim Hutchins
Chetfield Daily News · Sports Correspondent

CHETFIELD, OH – An official statement from the principal of Pickering High School (PHS) was released yesterday in response to the prank that took place on the campus of Chetfield High School (CHS) on the first day of school, which resulted in the injury of one of CHS's students. According to CHS principal, Bill Miller, the statement included an official apology to the Chetfield community. The statement also said an investigation was underway into the incident, and that when the perpetrators were found they would be turned over to the authorities.

"We at Pickering are deeply saddened by the actions of just a handful of students, and how those actions cast such a dark reputation upon our fine school and community," the statement read. "We offer our deepest apologies. The friendly rivalry between our two schools is one that has been enjoyed by many generations, and we look forward to many more years of friendship and cooperation as we educate the young people of Ohio."

The statement also included a strong warning about the upcoming Homecoming game between CHS and PHS, with admonitions against any kind of fighting, vandalism, or further pranks. Miller echoed those statements and has cautioned students of CHS against any retaliation.

"What was done by a few PHS students is wrong," Miller said. "The authorities will bring about justice in its due course. Any kind of retaliation by our students toward PHS would just be perpetuating more wrong. I beseech you to instead seek self-control and refrain from any kind of revenge. As the old saying goes: Two wrongs don't make a right."

The incident in question took place in the late afternoon on the first day of school. CHS freshman Chet Sayer said he saw five students on the CHS baseball field doing something with the Charlie the Chicken hawk mascot costume. As he approached the students, he noticed they were placing the costume on a scarecrow pole in the center of the field and spray-painting it blue and gold – the PHS colors. They also painted expletives onto the field, which CHS groundskeepers have been working to eliminate in the days since.

Sayer attempted to discourage the five boys who were vandalizing the field, but they overwhelmed him and beat him. A group of CHS football players saw the commotion and ran to Sayer's aid, chasing the PHS boys off. Sayer's wounds were minor – a noticeable black eye and some scrapes and bruises. He has spoken with authorities and described the physical attributes and limited information he has about the PHS boys. Sayer's first-person account of the incident can be found on The Scribbler's website.

The Homecoming game between CHS and PHS is slated to take place in two weeks.

CHAPTER 5

DEAD FISH

Chet set the newspaper down and then slowly folded it up, turning away from the poker table in front of him and tossing the paper onto an end table behind him. He was in the home of a senior named Jacob Matthews. It was Friday night, and he and Chunk had arrived at the house about 10 minutes earlier to participate in the weekly poker game they'd been invited to by Kevin and Steve. They'd been the first to arrive and were forced to wait for everyone else to show up – apparently arriving on time was a social faux pas and very "uncool," but as freshmen they hadn't known that. It was uncomfortable, as neither of them knew Jacob at all and he had only been notified an hour earlier that two freshmen would be joining the game that night. Chunk had been doing his best to engage Jacob in conversation, and Chet had noticed the town newspaper sitting on the end table and started reading to kill the time.

His first-person account of the prank had gotten more hits on The Scribbler website than any other story in the history of the paper. Dr. Delmar was singing his praises, much to Chet's embarrassment, and some of the other upperclassmen on the newspaper staff were treating him with professional respect. He felt good about himself, though Kaiah still seemed perturbed at him for some reason. Even Noélle – who typically seemed unaware of some of the social cues around her – seemed to recognize that Chet was building a bit of a legacy. She'd quipped the other day that he was setting the bar high for any future freshmen who might one day join The Scribbler staff.

"On the other hand," she'd said, "you're building quite a reputation for the News Hawks. The others kind of have to take us seriously now, don't they?"

Chet smiled as he reflected back on his first week. His editors – Sam and Liz – still didn't seem to like him much, but otherwise he'd made as much of a splash within the journalism program at CHS as he possibly could have. He knew it was a career he wanted to pursue, and he was proud of the strides he'd taken in just his first week. Things were looking good, and he felt an odd assurance that this evening at the poker game would help uncover more clues as to Gavin's disappearance. That was the premise under which he'd been allowed to come to the game. He'd somehow convinced his mom that he needed to interview the boys at the poker game for his continuing stories about Gavin. He wasn't quite sure she had bought it, but she'd let him come nonetheless.

It wasn't much longer before eight people were sitting around the poker table. In addition to Jacob, Chunk, and Chet, Kevin and Steve had arrived. Three other senior boys from the football team sat at the table, including the star quarterback, Aaron Johnson. He was a very tall black kid with a shaved head and wide-set eyes. Apparently, he and Chunk had developed a bit of a rapport over the course of football practices, as he was very friendly toward him despite their age differences. Then again, it was hard not to like Chunk. Nearly everyone got along with him. The other two boys at the table were Aaron's best friend and one of Jacob's friends. There was a ninth chair at the table still unoccupied.

Each person in the game was required to pay 20 dollars up-front, in exchange for a stack of different-colored chips that designated various denominations of bet sizes – from as little as five cents to as high as five dollars. There were two decks on the table, which were rotated from person-to-person in a clockwise manner, so that everyone shared equal responsibility for shuffling and dealing cards. The game they were playing was a popular poker game called Texas Hold 'Em, which Chet only vaguely knew how to play. He understood the basics – four rounds of betting, which hands beat which, and of course bluffing – but he didn't fully appreciate the nuances of the game. The older boys at the table were throwing around words like "nuts" and "donkey" and "dead fish" that made no sense to him whatsoever. They also had nicknames for certain hands, such as the "dead man's hand" or "flat tire" or "The Doyle Brunson."

While Jacob distributed the chips, Kevin explained to Chunk and Chet that there were two ways to play Texas Hold 'Em: a tournament style, where the top three players would win the total amount of money, or a cash game, in which anyone could "cash out" any time they wanted to. They were playing the latter because it allowed the people in the game to leave whenever they wanted. Apparently when the group decided to play a tournament it often extended into the late hours of the night – or early morning, as the case may be.

A random draw of cards made Chet the second person at the table to have to shuffle and deal. He was so nervous when his time came that he spilled the deck on the table on his first shuffle, then bent a handful of the cards on his second attempt. The creases were so bad that they had to replace the entire deck with a new one.

"Just wash them, dude," Aaron said gruffly, shaking his head at Chet's clumsiness. Chet just looked at him with a blank stare. "You know, wash them – lay them out face-down in front of you and mix them up while they're flat on the table. That shuffles them just as easy as anything else."

Chet smiled sheepishly and complied, then proceeded to deal the cards. He forgot to wait for the round of betting before putting out the three cards on the "flop," however, and had to start the entire process over again. His face was red from scalp to neck in embarrassment, and he could feel

Chunk shifting uncomfortably next to him. The other boys were snickering under their breath or sneering openly as they waited impatiently for him to get on with it and deal the cards. He wished desperately for someone to start a conversation about something that would distract the others from his ineptitude. Miraculously, Aaron came to his rescue.

"That's quite a shiner you've got there, Chet," he said, nodding toward Chet's black eye – which in the four days since his encounter with the Pickering boys had turned from purple to a sickly shade of brown and yellow. "Chunk told me about how you stood up to those Pickering jerks. Good for you!"

Chet beamed and sat up a little straighter.

"Thanks!" he said. "I honestly didn't think about what I was doing. Pretty stupid to try to take on five guys by myself. Chunk bailed me out, though. Kind of reminds me of the first day we met, right Chunk?"

"Ha! Yeah!" Chunk said, smiling broadly. "What would you do without me?"

Chet rolled his eyes at his friend, but smiled. He wasn't going to say it out loud, but he secretly loved that he had a best friend like Chunk who had his back. In his head he kind of thought of Chunk like a bodyguard, though one who was more of a best friend than someone who merely provided security.

"What's this?" Aaron asked. "What happened the first day you met?"

Chunk laughed and clapped Chet on the shoulder. Chet winced – it hurt every time Chunk did that.

"It was the first day of seventh grade," Chunk said, already chuckling about the story. "Chet and I were riding the bus to school and when we got up to get out, an idiot named Duncan stuck his foot out and tripped Chet. Fell right on his face. *SMACK*!"

The boys at the table chuckled, every one of them looking at Chunk with rapt attention as he wove his story, even Kevin and Steve who had already heard it. Chet just shook his head ruefully and smiled at the memory of what happened next.

"I didn't think that was a very nice thing to do to someone, so when Duncan stood up, I wiped that smug smile off his face by punching him right in the nose!" Chunk said, smiling broadly. He punched his fist into the palm of his other hand for emphasis. The boys at the table erupted in laughter, and Chunk reveled in their adoration. Chet smiled at him and couldn't help but join in the laughter.

"Serious?" Aaron asked after catching his breath, looking to Chet for affirmation.

"Oh yeah!" Chet said, nodding emphatically. "There was blood everywhere. We both got a day of in-house suspension for it and everything. That's when I gave Chunk his nickname. We started talking about movies and found out that we both like 'The Goonies.' I was stupid and blurted out, 'You look just like Chunk!' I thought he would punch me like he did Duncan, but he just started laughing."

Aaron smiled and nodded his head, looking back to Chunk.

"I like you Edwards," he said. "What do you say we win a state championship this year?"

"I'm game," Chunk replied immediately.

"Oh yeah!" Kevin said, pumping a fist in the air. "We're definitely gonna win this year! And Pickering better watch out cuz we're gonna crush them next week!"

Chet smiled as the rest of the boys gave their various proclamations of support, then finally dealt everyone their two cards to start the game. As Aaron looked at his two cards – one hand protecting them so no one else could see what they were – he glanced briefly at Chunk.

"You gonna come with us to the Pickering game tomorrow?" he asked Chunk. "We're gonna go scout them out. Coach VanDyne is gonna record the game so we can go over their formations at practice this week, but I want to see them in person."

Chunk nodded his head emphatically. "Yeah, I'd love to come," he said.

A thought flashed through Chet's brain and he spoke up.

"Can I come, too?" he asked quickly.

"I'm still investigating the disappearance of Gavin Brigantz, and the Pickering boys were the ones who found the Charlie costume. I'd like to see if I can dig up some more information."

Aaron smirked at him but nodded his head. "Sure," he said. "Might as well ride with us. Though I doubt the Pickering people will be glad to see the guy who ended up getting five of their starters benched for half the season."

Chet blinked and then realized that Aaron was right – if he showed up at the game the next day he'd have a target on his back, for sure. When he'd given his details of the incident to the authorities, he'd included the two names he'd heard – Dave and Jimmy. Combined with the descriptions of their physical characteristics, it hadn't been hard for the authorities to determine who the five boys had been. Chet, of course, was asked to confirm their identities when he was shown their pictures, which he had done without hesitation. All five of them, it turned out, were seniors and starters for the Pickering team. When Chunk had found out that the school had suspended them for a month and made it so they couldn't play for half the season – most specifically in the Homecoming game against Chetfield – he'd been ecstatic.

"It's alright, dude, I've got your back," Chunk said.

"Yeah … us too," Kevin said, glancing at Steve, who nodded his head and gave Chet a small smile.

"Thanks," Chet said, genuinely abashed. "I'd just like to ask around, you know? See if anybody knows anything else.

One of the guys who was holding my arms said they found the Charlie costume in a pile of trash by some old building. If Gavin had the costume last, knowing where those Pickering guys found it might give us a clue about where Gavin is or why he's missing."

No one said anything, and in the ensuing silence the older boys shared looks that Chet couldn't quite decipher – confusion, perhaps … or maybe a shared knowledge that didn't need words to be conveyed.

"Speaking of Gavin … it'll be nice to have a poker game without him for once, eh?" Aaron quipped, his dry chuckle breaking the silence. Chet looked up sharply in surprise, and then glanced around in more surprise as most of the boys laughed in response.

"For sure!" Jacob said. "A nice, peaceful game for once."

The other boys nodded in agreement. Chet looked at Chunk, who just shrugged his shoulders and shook his head. Aaron noticed their confusion, however, and explained what everyone else at the table took for granted.

"He's a jerk when he plays poker," Aaron said. "Most of the time he's fun to hang out with, and probably most people love being around him, but not when he's playing poker. He pushes buttons on purpose, and when he can tell that he's gotten under your skin he pushes even more."

Chet looked at Kevin and Steve and they shrugged uncomfortably while nodding in agreement with Aaron.

"It's a strategy," Steve said, shrugging again. "Some of the professionals use it because it makes other players emotional and they make mistakes. Maybe it works ... I dunno. Gavin swears it does. He said his dad goes to the casinos all the time and plays poker and it works for him. Though if that were true you'd think they'd have more money. Maybe you've heard but Gavin doesn't have the best home life. Both his parents are drunks and they're never around. He's always talking about running away when he gets old enough and moving to Vegas to be a professional poker player ... and, honestly, he does tend to win a lot when he plays with us, so maybe he could actually do good there."

"That's true," Jacob said. "He took quite a bit last time we played."

"Yeah, but he still owes Sam, like, 500 bucks, I think," one of the other boys said while glancing discreetly at his two face-down cards – the "hole cards," as the older boys had called them. It was the fifth time he'd looked at the cards in the minute since Chet had dealt them.

"Five hundred bucks?!" Chunk blurted out. "Sheesh! For what?!"

The other boy looked up with a half-grin and started to answer, but Aaron cut him off with a look.

"You'll have to ask Sam," Aaron said, nodding to the empty seat still at the table. "He should be here pretty soon."

Chet continued the next round of betting and dealing,

with five of the eight folding their hands. He was about to fold his own cards when he realized that Aaron might have been talking about his editor.

"Wait, Sam?!" Chet said louder than he meant to. "My Sam? I mean, my editor Sam?"

The other boys burst out laughing, and even Chunk joined them. Chet blushed again in embarrassment and impatiently waited for them to stop laughing at his expense.

"My Sam?" Kevin teased in a high-pitched voice mocking Chet's from a moment earlier. "I didn't realize you two were so close!"

That brought on another round of laughter, which Chet endured by gritting his teeth and staring at the poker chips in front of him. Eventually they controlled themselves, though there was a stray chuckle here and there.

"Yes, your Sam," Aaron said with a big grin, and more chuckles twittered around the table. "He doesn't like Gavin very much, but he loves to gamble and Gavin is always up for a big bet."

"What did they bet on?" Chet asked, pressing for information. Aaron just shrugged his shoulders and shook his head.

"Like I said, you'll have to ask him," the big quarterback said flatly, obviously indicating that he was done talking about it. Chet nodded slowly and finished dealing the hand. Steve ended up winning the chips from that round – the "pot," as they called it – and the game continued.

Chet chose to take a conservative approach and hardly played any hands. When he did play, he didn't bet a lot and often became intimidated when the older boys would raise his bets and put pressure on him. As a result, his chip stack was halfway depleted before he ever won a hand, and the pot he dragged didn't even come close to bringing him back to even.

About 30 minutes after they'd started the game, Sam arrived. He seemed preoccupied by something and barely gave a greeting to his friends before flopping down in the empty seat and tossing a 20 dollar bill on the table. He wore a stony look on his face and his eyebrows creased together creating a worry line down the middle of his forehead.

"Sorry I'm late guys," he said. "I had to run an errand. Took longer than I thought it would."

He spread a weak smile around the table, and as he did he noticed Chet and Chunk sitting at the table.

"What are you doing here, Lord Chetfield?!" he said with a sneer, not attempting to curb the contempt in his voice.

"I was invited, Sam," Chet said defensively, a hint of anger in his voice. He wasn't sure why Sam had such an aversion to him, but he didn't appreciate the downright disdain his editor showed every time they were in the same room together. "Kevin and Steve asked me and Chunk to come."

Sam looked to the two boys Chet had mentioned. Kevin

shrugged his shoulders and gave Sam a sheepish grin. Steve merely looked away and slouched down in his chair.

"Is there some problem here?" Aaron asked.

Sam looked at him for a long moment and then snorted.

"No," he said, flinging his hand up as if brushing away an unwanted pest. "Fine. Whatever. Let the celebrity freshman ride his 15 minutes of fame."

Sam crossed his arms and stared daggers at Chet while the next person at the table shuffled and dealt the new hand. Chet looked down at his cards and immediately threw them into the middle of the table to signify that he was folding.

"Any new word on Gavin?" Aaron asked suddenly, and it took a minute for Chet to realize he was looking at him. Chet blinked in surprise. "You said you wanted to ask around at the game tomorrow, but have you heard anything else this week?"

The quarterback looked briefly at Sam, who snorted in displeasure and then purposefully looked away. Chet shook off his surprise and replied.

"Nothing new," he said. "My friend Kaiah tried to talk to his mom, but she wasn't available. She went to Gavin's house yesterday and knocked on the door and some guy claiming to be Gavin's uncle answered the door. He said Gavin's mom was out looking for him and that the family wasn't talking to any reporters at the moment. I saw Jess in the hall yesterday between classes, but when I tried to ask her if she'd heard from Gavin she just started crying and ran off."

Chet shrugged and finished his story lamely, not knowing what else to say. Aaron looked at him for a long moment, then turned his gaze to Sam.

"And you haven't heard from him, either?" he asked Chet's editor. "I would have thought you'd want to know where he is, considering how your dad feels."

Sam glared at Aaron but didn't answer. Chet was confused by the comment.

"Plus, he owes you a lot of money, right?" Aaron pressed. "I mean, you can't hold out that much longer without that money, right? You-know-who is probably itching for his cut."

Sam looked at Aaron with hatred and slammed his fist down on the table, causing the neatly stacked chips to tumble into haphazard piles. Then he stood up suddenly and kicked his chair back.

"You've got a big mouth, Aaron," Sam said. He looked at the big quarterback for a solid five seconds, and Chet wondered if he was weighing the risk of further angering the much bigger boy. He must have decided against pushing his luck, however, as he didn't say anything more – just turned on his heel and walked out. He left behind his stack of chips and the 20 dollars.

"Who's You-Know-Who?" Chet asked into the ensuing silence. "What're you talking about? Sam's dad?"

Aaron considered Chet's questions, then shook his head

as if responding to some inner dialogue.

"Nothing," Aaron said. "Nobody. Just forget it."

"Are you suggesting Sam had something to do with Gavin's disappearance?" Chet pressed, and this time he received an angry look from the much bigger boy. There was a glint in his eyes that promised something more extreme if Chet didn't back off.

"I said forget it," he said flatly, and Chet flinched back. He nodded emphatically, and Aaron's gaze lingered for a long moment before he grabbed one of the decks of cards and started shuffling. "C'mon, let's keep playing. Jacob, turn on some music or something."

Jacob – who, like the other boys at the table, had been staring in shock at the door through which Sam had just left – jumped as if zapped and hurried over to a stereo. A moment later music was playing. It seemed to do the trick as the tension began to ease out of the room. As the game continued, nothing more was said about the incident and the laughter from earlier in the evening returned. But Chet couldn't stop thinking about what had happened and the things he'd overheard.

Is Sam involved with Gavin's disappearance? Does he know something? And why does Gavin owe him money?

He was so distracted the rest of the night that he ended up losing all the money he'd come with. When he complained about it to Chunk as they were leaving later, his friend just laughed in response.

"Face it, bro, that was gonna happen anyway," the bigger boy said. "You pretty much suck at poker."

Chet frowned, snorted at himself, and then joined his friend in laughing at their evening's adventures.

State Championship Aspirations Diminish In Wake Of Disciplinary Action

By Emily Edwards
Pickering Democrat · Staff Writer

PICKERING, OH – The hopes of a state football championship may have been dashed before the season even started, thanks to the actions of five senior starters for the varsity team at Pickering High School (PHS).

Earlier this week principal Anthony Cordello suspended five students who participated in a vandalism prank against rival Chetfield High School (CHS). Head football coach Dan Williams quickly followed that announcement with disciplinary action of his own, proclaiming that the five students in question would be denied from playing any games for the first half of the season – including the game at CHS, which is the biggest game of the year.

"I'm incredibly disappointed in the actions of these boys," Coach Williams said. "It was selfish and stupid, and it weakens our team considerably not to have the five of them on the field. But we are running a program of integrity here, and we will not allow such thoughtless action to go unpunished."

Coach Williams noted that the loss of these five players is particularly difficult to the team's strategy because all five of them were key starters in important positions. David Anderson is the starting middle linebacker and is instrumental in stopping opposing teams from running the ball effectively, Coach Williams said. Jimmy Gonzalez is also a starter on defense and the team's No. 1 safety, which Coach Williams said will be perhaps the biggest loss against CHS as the safeties will be needed to contain the effective rushing attempts for which CHS's quarterback, Aaron Johnson, is known. Brandon Brown and Alex Miller are both starting linemen and are key to helping the PHS offense run the ball well, not to mention protecting the quarterback when he drops back to pass. And finally, Nick Spencer is the team's starting wide receiver and perhaps the best player on the team. He is one of two players on the team with a strong chance to go on to play Division I football after graduation.

According to the public police report from the Chetfield Police Department, these five Pickering students vandalized the baseball field at CHS and attacked a freshman boy, injuring him. The freshman boy's family has chosen not to press charges, though the vandalism charge is a misdemeanor that could mean community service time for each of the five students.

"It's a black mark on the otherwise fine reputation of the Pickering High School football team," Cordello said. "We're proud of all of our sports teams, and we are hopeful that we can get past this experience and cheer our football team on to a good season."

The game against CHS is slated for 7 p.m. next Friday. It is CHS's Homecoming game and will take place on their school's campus.

CHAPTER 6

SWIMMING THROUGH THE WATER MAZE

The Pickering High School newspaper accidentally slipped out of Chet's hands and fell to the ground as he was jostled from behind by someone in the crowd at the PHS football stadium. He was standing in line at one of the concession stands with Chunk, who was already wolfing down one hot dog with his right hand while trying to hold two more in his left. The newspaper had come from a stack on the corner of the concession stand. The cover story featured mugshots of the five boys in question at the top. Chet couldn't help but smile in satisfaction after reading about the consequences of their actions.

"You like the story?" a girl's voice asked from in front of him, and when he stood up, he was looking into the blue eyes of a pretty, blond-haired girl. She was wearing a blue PHS shirt and had a blue-and-gold ribbon in her hair.

"What?" he blurted out, extending the newspaper as if offering it to her. She looked down at his hand in confusion and then back up to his eyes, a funny look on her face. "Uh… sorry. I don't know why I did that."

Chet hastily put the newspaper back on the edge of the concession stand and then shuffled his feet as he glanced at her. She was smiling at him now – it was a different kind of smile than Kaiah's, but no less beautiful. In fact, he was finding it difficult to think clearly as she stood there smiling at him.

"I said, do you like the story?" she asked again. "I wrote it, so I was just wondering if you liked it."

"You wrote it?!" Chet blurted, eyes wide. He glanced over at the newspaper and squinted to read the name on the story's byline. It said Emily Edwards. "You're … ah … Emily?"

She nodded at him confidently and smiled again, a little laugh escaping through her lips.

"Yeah … uh … I liked it," he said. "Nice work."

"Thanks," she said. "I'll take that as a compliment coming from the guy who seems to be a legend at Chetfield. I read your story, you know … the one about the missing boy. And I read your first-person account about the prank. You're a pretty good writer."

It took a minute for Chet to realize his mouth was

hanging open, and he shut it quickly with a noticeable *clack*! He winced, then processed what Emily had just said and stood up a little straighter, finally smiling back at her.

"Huh … guess I won't be flying under the radar like I'd hoped," he said, looking around to see if anyone else had overheard their conversation and now knew that he was encroaching on their turf.

"Yeah, it is a bold move coming here the same week that you get five of our most popular football players suspended from school," Emily said dryly, rolling her eyes for emphasis. She seemed the kind of person who spoke boldly without caring what other people thought. She kind of reminded him of Noélle. "What are you doing here, anyway?"

Chet looked over his shoulder at Chunk, who had finally managed to pay for his hot dogs and was starting to walk toward them. Chet noticed his friend had a box of peanut M&Ms sticking out of his pocket, too. Chet turned back to Emily and nodded his head toward Chunk as he answered her question.

"I came with some of our team," Chet said. "They wanted to see your team in person before we play you guys next week, and I wanted to see if I could maybe find out where those guys found our mascot costume. One of them – Jimmy, I think – said something about finding it in some junk at an old building. If I can figure out where that is, then it might give us a clue as to what happened to Gavin – the kid who's gone missing. He's our team mascot …"

Chet trailed off and shrugged at her, not knowing what else to say and afraid he'd already said too much. Maybe he shouldn't have told her why the CHS football team was there. It felt a little bit like spying, and he didn't want to be the one who accidentally ratted on Chunk and his teammates. Emily just nodded knowingly.

"Makes sense," she said. "Also sounds like the stories about you are true."

"Stories?"

"Yeah … that you're over-eager and don't stop digging until you get the story," she said. "Our journalism teacher even talked about you in class this week."

She rolled her eyes at that, but Chet couldn't help feeling a swell of pride. If teachers at other schools were talking about his reporting skills then he must be leaving a bigger impression than he realized. Kaiah was going to be furious!

"C'mon," Emily continued, tossing her head to the side and turning toward the walkway behind the bleachers. "I know someone who can probably answer your questions."

Chet took an involuntary step toward her, then had a second thought and looked around to see if Chunk was still there with him. The bigger boy was right behind him, licking ketchup off his fingers. He had one more hot dog left, and he seemed oblivious to the conversation Chet had been having with Emily.

"Don't worry," Emily said as if reading Chet's mind.

"No one is going to hurt you."

Chet gave her a sheepish look and then nodded. He quickly explained to Chunk where he was going and asked his friend to save him a seat in the stands, then he turned and followed Emily. Pickering was a large high school and boasted one of the largest non-college-affiliated stadiums in the state. There were bleachers on either side of the stadium, with the home team fans sitting on one side and the visitors on the other. Emily walked him behind the entire length of the home-team bleachers to the other side of the field, then turned a corner and walked up a ramp toward the field. Chet stayed by her side and tried to keep up – she was a fast walker. When they got to the end of the ramp, she signaled for him to stay where he was and she started up the steps of the bleachers, scanning the crowd for someone. Chet looked at the field and noticed the teams were about to begin. The head referee blew his whistle and the opposing team kicked off to the home team, starting the game. A loud cry rose from the crowd and Chet felt momentarily overwhelmed by all the noise.

Suddenly Emily was back beside him, and with her was another girl. She was shorter than Emily with olive-colored skin and dark eyes. She had long black hair that was pulled back into a ponytail, and she was looking at him with suspicious eyes. Emily motioned for him to follow her back down the ramp, and the other girl joined them until they were back in the relative quiet of the walkway behind the bleachers.

"Chet, this is Isabella," Emily said. "She's Jimmy's girl-friend."

"*Was* Jimmy's girlfriend," Isabella said. "We're done. He's an idiot."

Chet noticed a slight Hispanic accent in Isabella's voice, and he couldn't help but smile at her passion as she denied being in a relationship with Jimmy. The boy they were referring to was one of the five who had accosted Chet on the baseball field during the prank gone wrong.

"Nice to meet you," he said, holding out his hand. "I'm Chet Sayer."

Isabella looked at him in shock, then nodded slightly and hesitantly reached out her hand to grab his, shaking it weakly. She eyed his black eye and Chet detected a faint hint of a wince as she released his hand.

"Bella, Chet is investigating the disappearance of that boy over in Chetfield," Emily said. "He overheard something Jimmy said the other day and is here to follow up on it."

Emily looked at him and nodded approvingly, then crossed her arms and looked at Isabella expectantly. The other girl gave her a curious look, then turned to Chet and raised an eyebrow.

"Right … uh … yeah … um … Jimmy said he found our mascot costume in a bunch of junk by an old building," Chet said, fumbling with his words. "The thing is, the guy who has gone missing is the one who wears the mascot costume. His name is Gavin Brigantz, and he was the last person known to have had the costume. So, if I could figure out where Jimmy and his friends found the costume, it might give me a clue about what happened to Gavin, or where he is."

Chet shrugged and shuffled his feet as he looked at Isabella and held his breath, hoping she might know something. It had seemed like a long shot coming here for information about Gavin, but if Isabella could tell him where the boys had found the costume then it would turn into quite the fortuitous trip.

"I don't know where they found it," Isabella said, shrugging and looking down. "Jimmy said they were going to sneak onto your campus from the woods and spray paint your field. I didn't even know they had planned on doing anything to the mascot."

Chet chewed the inside of his lip and closed his eyes as he thought. He put the image of his school and the grounds around the building in his head, trying to picture the woods she was talking about. There were some woods adjacent to the baseball field, but they were nowhere near any roads. The only way the boys would have been able to sneak onto the campus from there would have been if they parked at the old water plant and walked about half a mile through the woods to the field – but that would have meant they had to slog through a marshy area around the creek. But it was the only thing Chet could think that fit with Isabella's information.

"The water plant!" Chet said. "That has to be it!"

Isabella looked at him curiously and shrugged again. Emily smiled at him and nodded encouragingly. He fleetingly wondered why she was helping him, but attributed it to the fact that she was another news person who had the itch for seeking out the truth of things.

"Thanks!" he said to both of them. "This helps a lot!"

Isabella smiled slightly at him, and he could tell she felt good about having helped in some way. Emily, too, stood a little taller and seemed pleased with herself. Chet said his goodbyes and then raced back around the bleachers to the concession stand where he'd left Chunk. He looked to his right and saw that the only way to the other side of the field and the opposing team's bleachers where his friends were sitting was along a narrow path that wound alongside the locker rooms.

About halfway down the path – just as he was passing the building that housed the locker rooms – Chet noticed a couple of people standing discreetly behind the smaller building, out of sight of anyone in the stands. They were talking heatedly, and the only reason they caught Chet's attention was because of how one of them kept looking over his shoulder as if wary of anyone seeing the two of them together. One of the men was tall and middle-aged, with silver hair and a salt-and-pepper beard. He wore a suit jacket and button-down shirt with no tie, khaki pants and shiny black boots. The other guy wore jeans and a light jacket, and when he turned his head again to look over his shoulder Chet was surprised to recognize him as Mr. Boreland, the CHS science teacher.

What's he doing here? Chet wondered.

He stopped walking and watched the two men as they continued their conversation. Mr. Boreland was very emphatic about whatever he was talking about – as if trying to convince the other man of something very important. He kept gesticulating as he talked, and the other man started to nod slowly, a flash of excitement crossing his face. After a minute, the taller man gave one strong, confident nod, smiled at Mr. Boreland triumphantly and then reached into his back pocket, pulling out his wallet. He fished in his wallet for some cash, then handed over some money. Chet wasn't close enough to see how much money was exchanged, but if those were one-hundred-dollar-bills then he'd just handed over quite a bit. Mr. Boreland put it in his own pocket immediately, glancing over his shoulder again. That's when he saw Chet standing there watching them.

Chet felt an immediate moment of panic. Mr. Boreland's face flashed shock, then anger, then determination as he glared at Chet. Without thinking, Chet took off and raced the rest of the way down the path and around the field, searching the opposing team's bleachers for Chunk and the other CHS football players. When he found them – sitting at the very top, of course – he bounded up the stairs and slid in beside Chunk. His friend was eating the peanut M&Ms.

"Want one?" Chunk asked, holding out the box to Chet, who shook his head.

"Dude, I just saw Mr. Boreland!" Chet said between heavy breaths.

Chunk glanced at him curiously, then down at the path that wound around the field that Chet had just walked along. Mr. Boreland wasn't there.

"OK …" Chunk said, clearly confused.

"I mean, it's weird, isn't it?" Chet said. "Why would he come here?"

Chunk shrugged. "Who knows? Maybe he just loves high school football."

"Ha Ha," Chet said sarcastically. "Very funny."

"Why do you care?" Chunk asked as he turned back to the football field and re-focused on the game.

"I dunno," Chet said, frowning at his friend. "He didn't seem happy to see me. I guess my radar is up with him considering what Kaiah said the other day about overhearing his phone call."

Chunk gave him the briefest of looks out the side of his eye, then shrugged again and continued to watch the game.

"OK, fine," Chet said, relenting. "I'm over-thinking it. Whatever. But guess what else? I figured out where those Pickering boys found the Charlie costume!"

"Cool," Chunk said with disinterest, barely paying attention as he watched the game playing out in front of them.

"Yes, it is cool," Chet said defiantly. "Very cool. I want to go check it out after this."

"Check what out?" Chunk asked, still only half paying attention.

"The old water plant," Chet said, grinning as he waited for the words to sink in.

Chunk didn't say anything at first. Then, it slowly dawned on him what Chet had said, and he turned to look his friend in the eyes. A slow frown spread across his face.

"The water maze?" Chunk asked, panic dancing in his eyes. "You want to go into the water maze?"

Chet just nodded, chuckling at the growing fear on his friend's face.

"You want to break into a place wired to explode?! … At night?!" Chunk asked, his eyes darting everywhere as he searched for something that would dissuade his friend.

Chet's smile started to crack, but he wasn't going to back down now. He took a deep breath and nodded once to his friend. Chunk's face fell, but he let out a loud sigh and slumped his shoulders before turning to the other boys.

"Hey, we're gonna explore the water maze after this, OK?" he said, spilling a couple of M&Ms. Kevin seemed confused for a moment, then adopted a pensive look and shrugged his shoulders.

"Sure," he said. "Sounds like fun."

Chet was annoyed by how underwhelmed Kevin seemed

to be, but he ignored it and turned to watch the game. It was
a lopsided match, with Pickering – one of the best teams in
the state – completely dominating the opposing team, despite being without five of its top starters. The longer the
game went, the wider the margin of victory became and by
the end of the third quarter the other boys were ready to
leave. It was dark by that time – nearly 9 p.m. – and Chet
wondered if the rest of them would be averse to exploring
the water maze at night. But when Chet brought it up again,
all of them seemed excited by the idea, much to Chunk's
chagrin. Chet joined Chunk, Kevin and Steve in piling into
Aaron's SUV and away they went.

It took a little more than 30 minutes to drive back to
Chetfield. By the time they arrived at the dirt road that
led into the water plant it was nearing 10 p.m. There was a
wooden blockade at the entrance of the old facility, and Steve
hopped out of the car quickly to slide it out of the way while
Aaron drove through. Steve then put the blockade back and
hopped back in the car. The dirt road to the old building
wasn't a long one, but it was overgrown with vegetation. The
trees and shrubs to either side of the road reached toward
them like the outstretched fingers of eager animals. In the
dark the headlights made odd-shaped shadows that lent an
ominous tone to their adventure.

When they pulled up to the building a minute later
Aaron parked right by the front entrance. The old building
was only one story and was far more wide than it was tall.
Broken windows lined the entire front of the building, and

ivy climbed the sides of the walls while branches from trees grown wild hung down and brushed the roof. It was already a dark night, and the thick vegetation blocked out what little light there was in the night sky.

"Does anyone have a flashlight?" Chet asked with a tremor in his voice. No one answered, but a moment later a bright light blinked on. Aaron was holding his cell phone in his hand and had activated his flashlight feature. The look on his face was clearly meant to belittle Chet, and the other boys chuckled. Chet felt his face flush as he reached into his pocket to pull out his own cell phone.

Aaron started forward toward the boarded-up front doors. There were warning signs put up on the columns that lined the front of the building, as well as across the front doors. Red wires crossed along the top of the doors and stretched along the top of the wall. The wires slipped through the tops of the front doors and continued inside. Chet remembered that the building was set to be demolished soon – though he couldn't remember the exact date – and that they'd been warned about exploring the building because of the dangers. Chet was fairly sure there weren't any live explosives set up yet, but seeing all the wires gave him second thoughts. He started to say something about turning back, but Aaron just shrugged and ripped the warning sign off the door and pulled on the handle. Surprisingly, the door opened with ease.

"Hold on," Chet said, and everyone's eyes swung to him.

"I want to look around the outside first. Jimmy – the Pickering boy – said they found Gavin's mascot costume here … I think."

Aaron stared at him for a long, drawn-out moment. Then he shrugged and started walking along the front of the building toward the corner. Chet hurried up beside him, and the other boys gathered around. The red wires continued around the side of the building and all along the entirety of the long wall. Chet assumed they went around the entire building.

"I bet there are coyotes out here," Chunk said suddenly, turning his flashlight to look into the woods.

"And lions and tigers and bears, too, I bet," Aaron sneered. The other boys chuckled while Chunk shot him a dirty look. Chet didn't laugh, though. He, too, felt nervous.

As they reached the corner of the building, Chet saw a huge pile of trash lining the edge of the building. It was long and wide and filled the 100 yards between the decrepit building and the creek that ran through the woods – the same creek the Pickering boys would have had to wade to sneak onto the Chetfield High School grounds. In the pile of trash was anything and everything – old tires and broken furniture and a molded-over refrigerator and a rusted-out barbecue grill and even an entire kitchen sink. Chet felt a rush of excitement, and he knew immediately this was where the Pickering boys had found the mascot costume.

"This has to be it," Chet said out loud.

"So what?" Aaron asked, looking at Chet with confusion. "So they found the Charlie costume here … what difference does that make?"

"It means Gavin was here," Chet said defensively.

"Or that the person who kidnapped him threw his costume here," Aaron said in response.

"Or maybe his body is in that pile of trash somewhere…" Steve said quietly. Everyone froze and looked at Steve in surprise.

"Well that's a cheerful thought," Kevin said sarcastically, frowning at his friend.

"Sorry," Steve said.

Hesitantly, Chet walked toward the edge of the trash pile, shining his light to look for clues. He began walking along the edge of the building toward the back, shining his light all along the refuse. He couldn't find anything that seemed to indicate any further clues about Gavin or why the costume would have been there. When he got to the next corner of the building, he looked over his shoulder and realized the other boys had walked with him the entire way.

"Well, don't stop now," Aaron said with a smirk. "Let's go all the way around."

Chet looked at him in surprise, then nodded and stood up straighter, trying to convince himself he was braver than he actually was. He looked out at the forest and jumped when he heard an owl hoot in the night. Chunk laughed at him, and he glared at his friend before putting his light in front of him and continuing forward.

At the back of the building they came across another set of doors, also with red wires slipping through the tops. But when Aaron tried to open them they wouldn't budge. He just shrugged and then waved his hand, motioning for Chet to continue circling the building. Other than darkness and thick vegetation, there was nothing very remarkable about the building. They circled around the last corner and made their way toward the front. Most of the windows were broken, and every once in a while one of the boys would shine a light into the interior to take a look. Most of the rooms were filled with rotted out old desks or chairs flipped on their sides, if they weren't completely empty. One of the rooms could have been an old laboratory, as there were broken glass beakers and what looked to be other random scientific tools strewn about. Chet didn't look too closely because the shadows inside made his skin crawl. He knew he was imagining things, but he kept envisioning creatures lurking in the dark hallways, and he swore at one point he heard a low wail from inside the building.

They were just about to come around the last corner at the front of the building when they all heard the sound of a car pulling down the dirt drive. Headlights flashed a moment later, and the five of them immediately flattened themselves against the wall, out of sight of whomever it was pulling up to the front of the building. Chet was still at the front of the group, and when he looked to the others he saw Aaron motioning to him frantically. Chet was confused at first, but then realized the older boy was trying to tell him to turn off his flashlight. Chet panicked and dropped his phone, making the light bounce around as it tumbled. He quickly bent down and grabbed his phone, clicking the button to turn off the light.

"Idiot!" Aaron hissed, and one of the other boys grunted in agreement. Chet just stood still and listened as hard as he could. A second later they heard a door close, which made Chet jump.

"I know you're here!" A man's voice rang out, and Chet jumped even higher. "Your car is still here. You might as well come out. You boys know you're not supposed to be here."

Chet looked at his friends and Aaron shook his head vehemently. He looked past Aaron to Chunk, who was also shaking his head. Chet held his hands up to them with a questioning gesture and then mouthed the words, "What do we do?" Aaron slowly leaned down to him and put his mouth right up to his ear.

"Sneak up to the corner and see who it is," he whispered almost imperceptibly into Chet's ear. Chet looked at him as if he were out of his mind, but Aaron put his hand on his shoulder and gave him a bit of a push. Chet swallowed hard and crept forward an inch at a time, slowly getting closer and closer to the corner of the building.

"There's no use hiding," The voice rang out again, and Chet flinched back. The voice sounded closer. "I saw your flashlight. I know you're here."

Chet looked over his shoulder and Aaron motioned him forward. Chet could just barely make out the older boy's face, and he wasn't giving him a very friendly look at the moment. Chet frowned back and then continued creeping forward until his face was at the very edge. Then, ever-so-slowly, he edged his head around and peeked one eye around the corner. Not 50 paces in front of him was Mr. Boreland, and he was walking toward their corner. Chet jumped back and scrambled toward the other boys.

"It's Mr. Boreland!" Chet whispered fiercely, rushing past the boys toward the back of the building, away from the approaching science teacher. "He must have followed us here from the football game! C'mon!"

After a moment's hesitation, the other boys started after him. All of them were football players in much better athletic condition than he was, and they quickly overtook him so that he suddenly found himself at the back of the pack, running as fast as he could. Before they were halfway down the wall, however, Aaron came to a sudden halt and then looked back over their shoulders. Chet stopped just before running into Chunk's back and looked over his shoulder, as well. Mr. Boreland hadn't turned the corner yet.

"C'mon, through the window," Aaron said quietly. "We'll lose him in the maze. Hurry!"

"Wait … WHAT?!" Chunk exclaimed, looking at the quarterback with panic-filled eyes. "I'm not going in there!"

"Fine," Aaron said as he started easing himself through the nearest window. "You can stay here and get caught. But if you rat us out, I'm gonna kick your butt."

Chunk shared a look with Kevin, who shrugged and immediately followed Aaron through the window. Chunk looked desperately at Chet, who shared the same trepidation about going inside the building. But he also didn't have a better idea at the moment. He tried to give Chunk a reassuring smile, then he jumped up and grabbed the edge of the window, flipping his legs up over the side and flopping unceremoniously into the room. A few seconds later Steve dropped down beside him, and Chunk followed last. Chet stood up and brushed himself off, then glanced quickly out the window. Mr. Boreland had turned the corner and was shining his phone light along the wall. Chet flinched back and ducked down.

"He's out there!" Chet whispered, backing away from the window in a kind of crab walk toward the door of the room. "Let's go!"

Aaron nodded and the five of them left the room in a rush. Once they were in the hallway, however, it was almost impossible to see. Chet couldn't even see his hand when he held it up in front of his face. He reached out his arms to try to find the walls, and his finger poked something wet.

"OW!" Chunk said. "That was my eye!"

"Sorry," Chet said lamely. "I can't see anything."

"Yeah, me either," Chunk said. "How are we gonna get out of here?"

"We go this way," Aaron said from off to their right. "It's toward the front. I'm gonna turn on my flashlight but try to keep it covered as much as possible. You guys keep yours off."

A moment later Aaron's light flashed on, though he covered it quickly with his hand. The dim light revealed more of the red wires snaking along the floor of the hallway, and when Aaron raised the light Chet could see that even more wires were attached to the ceiling in a kind of zig-zag pattern. The voice of their social studies teacher, Mrs. Whisman, echoed in his head: "…the massive concrete structure would crush you."

"Watch out for the wires!" Chet whispered urgently. "Don't trip on any of them. They might set off an explosion and then we'd be buried."

"What?!" Steve exclaimed. "There's no way they've got live explosives hooked up in here! I don't even think that's legal!"

"Do you know that for sure?" Chet asked. "Do you really want to risk it?"

Everyone stood frozen in place, looking at Chet with faces full of fear. All except Aaron, who straightened his shoulders and adopted a determined look. He shone his hooded light along the floor in front of them to check for more wires and started to slowly make his way forward. Chunk groaned.

Aaron's light was enough for them to see his silhouette, and the longer they crept through the hall the more Chet's eyes adjusted to the low light and he could make out more of his friends' features. Suddenly they heard a sound from the room behind them, and Chet realized Mr. Boreland was outside the window they'd just climbed through.

"Quit running!" the teacher yelled. "Be men and face the consequences of your actions! You don't want to get lost in here."

Chet jumped, and Chunk pushed him from behind toward Aaron, who started rushing down the hallway. Chet followed as quickly as he could, and a few steps later Aaron turned left and was winding through the aptly named water maze.

"Careful!" Chet whispered fiercely. "Watch your steps!"

Aaron shied back from the edge of the wall and the wires along the floor, but didn't slow down. Chet tried to keep up with him while watching where his feet were going. It was difficult, and he knew it had to be even harder for Kevin, who was at the back of their line.

Chet wasn't sure how long they walked through the halls of the building, but it felt like an eternity. Unlike other office buildings, this building didn't have any long halls. Instead, each hallway was only about 20 paces before it bent or turned a different way. It was unnerving having to stop at so many corners and hold his breath for fear of what might be around the next bend. He wondered absently if someone were to slice the roof off the building and take a picture from the top down if it would look like one of those mazes his mother had given him when he was younger … one of the more challenging mazes. It made him consider the architect who had designed the building and whether or not there was actually a hidden clue to the fabled treasure. He itched to search the halls for some clue as to what his father had been investigating.

Sometimes when they would come across an intersection of hallways there would be so many wires crisscrossing their path that they'd have to very carefully step between the wires while Aaron stood to the side shining his light down. One time while Chet was waiting for the others to finish tiptoeing through the wires, he saw a yellow rectangular box duct-taped to a column. Each of the corners of the intersection had a column, and when Kevin had finished maneuvering the maze of wires at his feet Chet hissed at them to stop for a second and motioned for Aaron to shine his light toward the ceiling. A second later his suspicions were confirmed – there were yellow boxes on each of the four columns, and the wires attached directly into their ends.

"Explosives!" Chunk hissed, and when they looked at each other Steve had such wide eyes and a look of fear on his face that Chet wondered how his own face must look at the moment.

"Calm down," Aaron said forcefully. "That's just the electric boxes. They haven't brought in the explosives yet."

"How do you know?!" Steve asked. "There could be explosives in those boxes!"

"You said it yourself," Aaron replied. "It wouldn't even be legal. They don't put the explosives up until the very last minute."

"So, you're an expert on demolition now?!" Steve pressed.

Aaron just glared at him while the rest of them stood frozen in place, not daring to move and risk hitting one of the wires.

"Better safe than sorry," Chet whispered emphatically. "Don't trip on any of the wires!"

Each of them looked at him for a long moment, then nodded.

They continued on their way, but now they were moving very cautiously … and slowly. Chet wondered whether Mr. Boreland would be able to navigate the maze any quicker than they were, but he didn't spare an extra thought for it as he concentrated on avoiding the wires. After a few minutes of scrambling through the halls, Kevin whispered up at them to stop.

"I think I heard something," he said harshly.

"Yeah, Mr. Boreland!" Aaron said angrily. "Keep moving."

"I think it was something else," Kevin said with a shaky voice. "It sounded like a moan or something."

Chet shot a startled look at the older boy, though he

couldn't see his face in the darkness. Chunk was breathing harshly beside him.

"Probably the ghosts," Aaron said cruelly, and when Chet looked toward him, the covered light from his phone set his face into such sinister shadows that he looked positively evil. "Let's go!"

"Do you know where we even are?" Chet asked, grabbing the quarterback's muscled arm before he could start walking again. "How do you know we're going the right way?"

Aaron frowned at him and shook his arm free. "I'm good with directions," he said confidently. "I'm pretty sure the front door is in this direction. Just keep moving."

As if to emphasize his words, a noise came from the hallway behind them that was distinctly running footsteps. It sounded like Mr. Boreland was gaining on them.

"Run!" Aaron hissed, and he turned and rushed off.

Chet raced after him frantically, not wanting to lose the light and desperate not to be left alone in the creepy water maze. Moving that quickly in the low light made it nearly impossible to watch where his feet were going, and he hoped desperately that he wouldn't trip on any wires. He could hear Chunk huffing along behind him, and he hoped the other two boys weren't far behind. The race through the halls was frantic, and Chet stopped jumping at every little shadow as he concentrated on keeping up with Aaron – his eyes focused on the older boy's back. When they passed open doorways on either side of the halls, Chet tried not to think about what kinds of creatures might be hiding inside. And occasionally when he imagined hearing strange noises it lent an extra burst of speed to his steps.

A loud thump suddenly sounded behind them, followed by someone cursing. Everyone stopped and Aaron shuffled back to them quickly, shining the light behind but still hooding it with his hand.

"What happened?!" he hissed.

"Kevin tripped over one of the wires!" Steve said in a high-pitched wail.

Everyone froze. Chet looked up at the ceiling as Aaron shined his light above them. All they could see were wires and none of the rectangular boxes. Chet looked down at the floor and didn't see any boxes there, either. Kevin started to slowly pull himself up off the ground, and Chet held his breath as the big lineman very carefully extricated his foot from two red wires that had become twisted around his ankle. From what Chet could tell it didn't look like Kevin had broken any of the wires, and since nothing had exploded yet he assumed they might be OK. It seemed to take Kevin forever to get his foot free, but Chet wasn't about to rush him. Finally, he got free and looked up at them, smiling widely. A moment later footsteps clearly sounded from the hallway behind them and Kevin's smile froze, replaced immediately with wide eyes and a look of terror.

"Run!" he mouthed.

They took off running again. Mr. Boreland was so close now, and Chet was sure they were about to be caught. He just kept running, though, his eyes fixed on Aaron's back as the bigger boy took long, confident strides through the hallway.

Suddenly they turned a corner and found themselves in a wide, open lobby with a wall of broken windows at the front of the building. Miraculously Aaron had led them through the maze to the main entrance, just as he had promised. He looked over his shoulder at them triumphantly, then crept to the front window nearest the door and peered outside cautiously. He looked around outside for a long moment, then looked back at the rest of them.

"I don't see anybody out there," Aaron said. "He must have come alone. C'mon, let's get out of here!"

None of them argued with him, and the five of them rushed through the doors to his SUV. They jumped in quickly and Chet winced at the loudness of Aaron's car engine revving up. That was a dead giveaway to Mr. Boreland that they were making a break for it. Aaron put the vehicle in gear and tore off down the dirt drive. Chet looked over his shoulder through the back window but never saw any sign of Mr. Boreland as they sped away. When they got to the entrance where the wooden blockade was, Chet was relieved to see that it was pulled to the side of the road. They wouldn't have to stop and move it, wasting valuable time to get away.

When they pulled off onto the paved road, they were all silent, the only sound between them the heavy breathing as they labored to recover from the run through the halls. Then suddenly Aaron broke the silence with a loud laugh, startling them all and making Chet jump yet again. A moment later they all started laughing with him, even Chet, who couldn't seem to make himself stop. He didn't feel any sense of mirth whatsoever, but the relief at getting free from such a dicey situation seemed to rush out of him with each successive laugh.

"That was close," Chunk said with a broad smile.

"Yeah …" Chet wheezed. "… too close. And I didn't even get to look for any clues about my dad."

Chunk's smile faded as he looked with pity on his friend.

"Sorry dude," he said.

Chet just shrugged and looked away, watching the trees pass by outside. It was yet another disappointing dead-end in his father's mystery, and on top of that he hadn't really learned anything new about Gavin's disappearance. All in all, the night felt like a waste.

Chetfield High School Staff Biographies:

Micheal Boreland, Science Teacher

Mr. Boreland earned his Bachelor of Science and Master of Science degrees from Ohio State University. Immediately following the completion of his degrees, he was hired as a government contractor studying molecular biology and ecology in labs in New Jersey and Maryland. After two years working in the government sector, Mr. Boreland moved back to Ohio and served in the science department at the University of Cincinnati. After nearly 13 years as a professional scientist, he decided to leave the lab and pursue another of his passions – teaching! He has been at Chetfield High School for five years.

Mr. Boreland maintains many professional and personal connections to the scientific community and is known around CHS for his willingness and enthusiasm in using those connections to help further his students' education. He also has many connections in professional sports, as he has served as a consultant for many medical staffs of professional teams. He is close personal friends with the general manager of the Cleveland Browns.

Mr. Boreland is an exacting teacher who demands excellence and attention to detail from his students, and yet shows grace to those students who prove they will work hard and try their best. When he isn't teaching biology, anatomy and physiology, he enjoys watching and playing sports – especially football and baseball – as well as kayaking and horse racing.

In addition to serving as one of the school's science teachers, Mr. Boreland is an assistant coach for the baseball team and is an active fan of all school sporting events, often seen in the stands at many CHS games rooting for his students.

CHAPTER 7

PIECES OF THE PUZZLE

Chet shook his head ruefully and handed Noélle's phone back to her. After sharing their experience from Saturday night with Kaiah and Noélle, Chunk and Chet had started asking questions about Mr. Boreland. Noélle had simply looked up his bio on the school website and handed him the phone to read.

"Sounds like a teacher," Chet said dryly. "Boring and bland."

"That's what people call him," Noélle said as she tucked her phone into a pocket. "Mr. Boring."

Chunk chuckled and Noélle smiled, while Kaiah continued to give Chet the cold shoulder. Her arms were folded, and she was slouched down in her seat, her face turned away from him and pointedly staring in front of her. They were in the study hall portion of their two-hour class on Tuesday and were comparing notes on their various investigations. Kaiah had seemed genuinely interested in his story about the poker game and Sam, but when he had mentioned his run-in with Emily and Isabella at the football game her face had turned blank. Then when Chunk had started talking about their adventure at the water plant – embellishing most of the tale along the way – her face had gone all stormy and she'd refused to look at him.

"Oh, c'mon Kaiah," Noélle said with a snort, slapping the other girl on her shoulder and making her flinch. "So they went into the water maze. Who cares? They got out OK and nothing happened."

Kaiah blinked at her and then frowned, then took a deep breath and slowly sat up. She turned purposefully toward Chet and he could tell she was trying hard to control her facial features – anger and determination warring with forced friendliness. The result was a look that made her seem as if she was about to be sick.

"Obviously Mr. Boreland is involved in Gavin's disappearance," Kaiah said matter-of-factly, as if it was a foregone conclusion that the rest of them would agree. But Chet did not agree, and he said as much.

"Oh, come on," Kaiah insisted. "First, I hear him yelling at somebody on the phone about owing him money, then you see him at the Pickering football game demanding money from what sounds like another teacher at that school. Then he follows you to the water plant, where you've confirmed that Gavin was sometime before his disappearance."

Chet squirmed uncomfortably in his chair and shot a look at Chunk, who just shrugged at him and took a bite of a power bar he'd brought from home.

"Technically I didn't confirm that," Chet said, holding his hands up quickly to stop Kaiah's retort. "At best I'm fairly certain that's where the Pickering boys found his mascot costume. Someone else could have put it there."

"That's what Aaron said," Chunk said innocently.

"Yes ... thank you Chunk," Chet said, frowning at his friend. "The point is that I *think* that's where Gavin was, but I don't know that for sure."

Kaiah started to object again, and again Chet raised his hands to ward her off.

"I'm also not convinced Mr. Boreland didn't just follow us there from the football game," Chet said. "He seemed pretty angry that I'd seen him exchanging money with that other guy, and he probably just saw us leave the game and decided to follow us."

"Yes, but *why*?" Kaiah said before Chet could stop her. "Does that even make sense? Why would a teacher follow you just because you saw him talking to another teacher? I mean ... who does that?"

Chet started to respond, then frowned and looked at Noélle. She smiled and nodded, indicating that she agreed with Kaiah. He looked to Chunk, who also nodded.

"She's got a point," he said with a shrug.

Chet sighed and shook his head.

"I think he saw us leave and decided to follow us. I don't know why," Chet said stubbornly. "Maybe he was about to leave the game, too. It was pretty much over by that point anyway."

He looked to Chunk for confirmation, who shrugged again and nodded in agreement.

"So maybe he just happened to be driving the same way we were going because we were all driving back to Chetfield," he continued, stubbornness digging in deeper. "And when he saw that we were going into the water plant he thought he would catch some students doing something wrong. Why would he have anything to do with Gavin's disappearance?"

"There could be a million reasons," Kaiah said. "We don't have enough information at the moment to put all the pieces together."

She looked at him with determination and he sighed in resignation. She might be right – it was odd for Mr. Boreland to follow them from the football game. But he still wasn't convinced Mr. Boreland was guilty of anything. He had to admit, though, it was strange what he'd witnessed between the science teacher and the PHS teacher at the football game.

"Whatever," he said. "Let's table that until we have more information. What did you two find out? Kaiah, any luck with Gavin's family?"

Kaiah sat up quickly and leaned forward, a smile spreading across her face and her eyes dancing with excitement.

"Yes, actually!" she exclaimed. "I talked to his mom!"

"Really?" Chet asked, equally excited and leaning forward in his chair. "How'd you manage that?"

"You're not the only investigative reporter with skills, Lord Chetfield," Kaiah said teasingly. "I can be relentless when I need to be. I basically camped out in front of Gavin's house this weekend and kept knocking on the door and being a general nuisance. She finally came home late Sunday afternoon."

"And what … you just walked up to her and said, 'Hi. I'm Kaiah. Do you know where your son is?'" Chet asked skeptically.

"No!" Kaiah said with a scowl. "I have more tact than that, thank you very much. I waited a few minutes after she got home, then politely knocked on the door – again – and asked Eric – that's Gavin's uncle – if she was home and whether I could talk to her. He wasn't very happy to see me – again … it might have been the twentieth time I had knocked on the door – but she overheard me and told him to let me in."

Chet couldn't help getting a little excited, and he leaned even closer as Kaiah continued.

"She's been all over the state, and even went down into Kentucky," Kaiah said. "Apparently her ex–boyfriend – one of

145

many guys she's dated since divorcing Gavin's dad – lives in Lexington and she wondered if maybe Gavin had gone down to be with him. Apparently out of all the guys she's been with, this one was the one Gavin got closest to. She started naming off all the guys she's been with and I seriously started feeling sorry for Gavin. I mean, his dad is a drunk and his mom has brought a parade of guys into the home!"

"So maybe he just ran away," Noélle speculated.

"I thought the same thing," Kaiah said. "Especially since the most recent guy really didn't get along with Gavin. Apparently, the police were called to their house three weeks ago because of a domestic dispute. Gavin's mom wouldn't tell me very much about it, so I went to the police station after I interviewed her and looked up the police report. Gavin and the guy his mom has been dating got into a fist fight. Nothing really came of it, though. No one was arrested or anything. But, I mean, if I were in Gavin's shoes I'd probably want to run away. And his mom told me he actually did run away once about two years ago. But it was only for a night, and he ended up spending the night with a friend because his mom and her boyfriend at the time had been having a big argument."

"Sheesh," Chet said. "Are we sure he didn't just run away?"

"I bet he did," Chunk said, chiming in. "Remember what the guys said at poker night about him wanting to go to Vegas. I bet he ran away and took a bus to Vegas or something."

Chet looked at his friend and contemplated what he said. It made sense, considering this new information Kaiah had brought to the table. It didn't sound like Gavin's home life was all that great, and running off to Vegas might have seemed like a great escape to him, especially if he had multiple people chasing him down because he owed them money. Chet almost wanted to believe it, but the memory of Jess crying in front of the police officers kept nagging at him.

"It's possible," Chet said. "But I'm not convinced yet. What else did his mom tell you, Kaiah?"

"Well, turns out the ex-boyfriend in Kentucky was a dead end," she said. "Gavin isn't there. She's been checking out other random places that she knows Gavin likes to visit – his favorite camping spot, a couple amusement parks, some of the bigger malls, that kind of stuff. She seemed pretty tired and worn down, actually. But she was adamant that he hadn't run away. She really believes something has happened to him."

Kaiah stopped long enough to reach into her backpack and pull out a notepad. She also pulled out her phone and tapped it while looking into Chet's eyes.

"I recorded the entire interview," she said. "It's on my phone. She has some good quotes we can use for the next story. The biggest piece of information, though, is that the guy she's been dating for the past three months – the guy Gavin got into a fight with – is Sam's dad!"

147

Kaiah dropped that bomb and then sat back with a satisfied smile on her face. Chet blinked and let her words sink in. Noélle let out a little whistle, and Chunk looked at them all with a slightly confused look on his face until he finally put the pieces together, then his eyes got wide and he sat up straight.

"That might explain why he got so mad at the poker game on Friday," Chunk said, looking at Chet. "I thought that was a little weird. I mean, he was way too mad just from a couple of comments from Aaron. Obviously there was something else there to set him off."

Chet nodded in agreement.

"You're right," he said. "If his dad and Gavin's mom were starting to get close, Sam probably wasn't too happy about it."

Chunk nodded, but when Chet looked at Kaiah she seemed skeptical.

"I don't think that's it," Kaiah said, obviously unconvinced. "You guys said Sam got mad when Aaron said something about Gavin owing him money."

"Yeah, 500 bucks!" Chunk said loudly, causing some of the other students near them to turn their heads.

"Why don't you talk a little louder, Chunk," Chet said sarcastically. "I don't think the people downstairs heard you."

"Sorry," Chunk said sheepishly.

"My point is, it sounds like Sam was more upset about

the money than he was about his dad dating Gavin's mom," Kaiah said. "When I asked her whether she'd checked with Sam's dad to see if Gavin was at their house, she brushed it off. She'd called him first after Gavin went missing, and he apparently didn't know anything about it. She seems certain Sam's dad didn't have anything to do with anything. She told me he was out of town that weekend, anyway."

"Where was he?" Chet asked.

"Playing poker," Kaiah said with a little laugh. "She said that's his only vice, and that he drives to one of the casinos most nights to play poker."

"Does she know for sure that he actually went to the casino?" Chet asked. Kaiah frowned and thought for a second, then hesitantly shook her head no.

"I see what you're suggesting," she said. "I suppose it's not a rock-solid alibi … at least, not until we can call the casino and confirm that he was there."

Chet nodded, mulling over this new piece of information. "Any idea what kind of guy Sam's dad is? Any reason to suspect he could be involved?"

Kaiah shook her head and looked down at her notes.

"Other than that fight with Gavin that led to the police being called, Gavin's mom said he's a good guy who takes good care of her," she said. "From what I can gather he likes to drink, but so does she. The bottle of wine she was drinking while we talked was gone by the time I left. Overall, I didn't get the impression from her that he was a bad guy. Just maybe a little rough around the edges. About the only thing that makes any kind of connection is the poker angle."

Chet looked at Chunk, who seemed contemplative. Noélle was fiddling with one of her braids as she considered Kaiah's information.

"Poker and gambling and money," Chet said. "That seems to be coming up a lot."

"That's true," Kaiah said. "What are you thinking?"

"I dunno," Chet said, looking out the window as he searched for elusive pieces of the puzzle. "Always follow the money …"

"What was that?" Kaiah asked.

"You haven't heard that quote?" Chet asked, turning back to them. "It's from 'All The President's Men.' One of my all-time favorite movies. You know, Deep Throat and Woodward and Bernstein and Watergate. Their source tells them to follow the money and it will lead them to all the answers. Most reporters use it as a mantra when they're investigating something."

Kaiah gave him a quizzical look and Noélle let out a little laugh. Chet looked at Chunk, who just shook his head ruefully and gave him half a grin.

"I think we should start trying to follow the money," he said, more confident now. "We know that Gavin owed Sam some money, and we know that he won some money at a poker game. We know that Mr. Boreland was yelling at someone to give him money – and yes, Kaiah, I see that look on your face and I guess I've come to your side. Maybe Mr. Boreland is involved somehow."

Kaiah gave him a satisfied smile and crossed her arms confidently.

"I just don't know how Sam's dad and Sam and Mr. Boreland and Gavin all fit together," Chet said. "And none of the things we know helps us understand any better why Gavin disappeared or where he went after football practice that day."

"Oh, I might know that!" Noélle said, chiming into the conversation for the first time. "I talked to Aaron Johnson's girlfriend and she said he wasn't happy with Gavin the day after he disappeared. This was before they knew he was missing, of course. Apparently, Gavin was supposed to have met with Aaron and a couple other people the night before to settle a debt. She didn't know who, but maybe it was Sam. Anyway, Aaron was mad because Gavin didn't show. They were supposed to meet at the gas station around the corner from the school. Apparently, Aaron saw Gavin riding his bike past the gas station. He knew it was him because the Charlie costume was tied to his back. I guess Aaron ran out of the gas station and yelled at him, which spooked Gavin and he took off on a little trail into the woods."

Chet blinked in shock and looked back and forth at Chunk and Noélle wonderingly.

"The woods on the other side of the baseball field?" Chet

asked, waving his hand toward the window and the old water plant in the distance. "Did Aaron chase after him?"

Noélle shook her head and frowned slightly.

"It has to be those woods," she said. "They're the only woods by the gas station. But no, Aaron didn't chase after him. His girlfriend said he planned on confronting Gavin after the next practice on Saturday, but he never showed up … and obviously we know that he disappeared before that. She said Aaron was genuinely surprised that Gavin was missing, so I don't think he had anything to do with it, if that's what you're thinking."

Chet nodded slowly and then looked meaningfully at Chunk. When his friend saw the look in Chet's eyes, he immediately started shaking his head.

"Absolutely not," Chunk said. "I will not confront the star quarterback on a hunch just so you can have a story for the newspaper. Not gonna happen."

"Oh c'mon," Chet said. "I thought you wanted to be one of the News Hawks."

"That's not fair," he said defensively, glaring at his friend. "Do you know how rare it is for a freshman rookie to get to hang out with seniors – especially the star of the team?! It. Never. Happens. I'm probably the first one in a hundred years. I'm not going to ruin that, dude!"

"Can't you just kind of innocently bring up the poker game from last Friday?" Chet pressed. "Just mention something in passing and do a little fishing for information. See if he knows why Gavin owed Sam so much money."

Chunk's glare deepened and he slunk down in his chair, crossing his arms and looking purposefully away from Chet in a manner that was almost the exact replica of Kaiah's posture from earlier. Chet couldn't help but laugh. After a long moment, Chunk gave one hesitant nod, and Chet considered that to be a victory.

"Great," Chet said, turning back to the girls. "Nice work everybody. I think the pieces are starting to come together. A little more digging and we might figure this thing out before Homecoming this weekend."

"Speaking of Homecoming," Noélle said playfully, "the dance is this Saturday night. You better hurry up and ask somebody."

"I'm only a freshman," he said, immediately uncomfortable. "I wasn't planning on going to the dance."

"Really?" Noélle asked, smiling mischievously. "That's too bad. I know someone who will be very disappointed to hear that."

Chet looked at her in confusion, and she very intentionally and slowly turned her head toward Kaiah, who was pretending not to pay attention while she started packing her things into her backpack. The class was about to end. Chet knew she'd heard everything, however, and that she was fully aware of what Noélle was implying. His discomfort increased tenfold and he felt a cold sweat start at the base of his neck and on his hands. Before he could think of anything to say, however, Chunk spoke up.

"Maybe you should ask that girl you met at the Pickering football game," Chunk said mercilessly. Chet's head popped up and he saw a wicked gleam in his friend's eye. "What was her name? Emily, I think? You know, the pretty blond girl with the blue eyes you kept talking about on the ride home. Sounds like she had a thing for you. I bet she'd go to the dance if you asked her."

Chet was mortified and his face had to have gone through five shades of red. He didn't have the courage to look at Kaiah, and instead stared furiously at his friend, who just grinned evilly back at him. He took a couple of deep breaths and worked up his courage before finally turning back to Kaiah. She was already up and out of her chair and halfway to the door of the classroom. She didn't look back once as Chet watched her walk away.

"Thanks, pal," Chet said, throwing Chunk a disappointed glare.

"Any time," his friend said, slapping him hard on the shoulder.

Chet winced. He really hated it when Chunk did that.

Lack of Evidence Toward Foul Play Leads Police to Speculate Brigantz Ran Away

By Chet Sayer and Kaiah Dufresne
The Scribbler · Reporters

CHETFIELD, OH – Police investigations into the disappearance of Chetfield High School senior Gavin Brigantz have yielded no results in the two weeks since his missing person's report was filed, leading many to speculate he merely ran away.

According to Detective Joseph Hastings, no evidence of foul play has been discovered. Hastings said the investigation has included multiple interviews with all members of Brigantz's family, his closest friends, school officials and teachers, and even witnesses throughout town with knowledge of his last-known whereabouts. Hastings also said officers have canvassed all parts of the town – including the woods nearby the high school – with no results.

Hastings said the biggest part of the investigation involves Brigantz's family. The most recent living situation for Brigantz included him living at home alone with his mother, Anita Brigantz. His father, Eddie Brigantz – who has been divorced from Anita for seven years – also lives in town and shares custody. Anita Brigantz has had multiple boyfriends in the seven years since her divorce, and Hastings said every one of them was interviewed and thoroughly vetted, with none of them having any evidence of being involved with Gavin's disappearance. Both Anita and Eddie Brigantz have previously admitted to problems with alcohol over the years, and Eddie told officers that he was passed out on the night of Gavin's disappearance, indicating that he has no memory of that evening.

"When there is literally no evidence to indicate a crime was committed, and when that lack of evidence is paired with an 18-year-old boy who is forced to live in a less-than-ideal home situation, the logical conclusion is that he just ran away," Hastings said. "That's the case nine times out of 10. He's an adult now, and he certainly wouldn't be the first young man to run away from a rough home life."

Though Hastings' opinion is one shared by many, Anita Brigantz insists her son has not run away and that something bad has happened.

"He wouldn't just run away," Anita Brigantz said. "He just wouldn't. I know this isn't the best place to live and things have been rough lately, but he wouldn't just leave without letting me know. He would have told me something! That's why I know something bad has happened."

According to Hastings, missing person reports are left open until either a body is located, or law enforcement officials make contact with the missing person. Hastings said it is not against the law to be a missing person and that if Gavin Brigantz wishes to remain anonymous, he is well within his legal rights to do so. That said, Hastings also encouraged anyone who has knowledge of his whereabouts or facts behind his disappearance to come forward.

CHAPTER 8

THE PAPERBOY

Chet threw down the paper in disgust. Not only had Sam buried his story about Gavin on the bottom of page three, but he'd also heavily edited it to the point that – in Chet's opinion – it basically encouraged people to believe that Gavin had run away.

Chet didn't know what to believe. What had seemed like a big mystery that needed to be solved now felt more like a muddled mess of misinformation that could ultimately be much ado about nothing. The more and more he dug, the more and more it seemed plausible that Gavin really could have run away. And now that they were two weeks into the investigation with no clear evidence of foul play, Chet couldn't think of any way to move the story forward.

He stood there looking at the stack of papers, trying to

muster up the motivation to take them to the newspaper racks around the school. The rookies on the newspaper staff – the freshmen – were required to distribute each week's newspapers to specific locations around the school before classes started on Friday mornings. The paper was completed on Thursdays and sent to a local printer, and the freshmen were supposed to pick up the freshly printed papers first thing on Friday mornings and distribute them around the school before students and teachers arrived. Noélle had done it the first week, and now it was Chet's turn. He wasn't much of a morning person as it was – most mornings his mom had to drag him out of bed – and having to get up an hour earlier than normal wasn't helping his grumpy disposition.

He sighed and then shrugged his shoulders in resignation. Then he stacked the papers into a vertical pile on a dolly that he could wheel around the school. There was approximately 30 minutes for him to make it around the school before students started arriving. As he wheeled the dolly out of the newspaper room, he noticed there were more lights on than when he had first arrived. Teachers and school administrators were arriving. This was confirmed when he dropped off the first stack of papers to the school office and saw the assistant principal walking down the hall toward her office.

He continued down the main hall to the large common area, adding a stack of papers to the newspaper rack that sat against the wall in the atrium. Then he made his way farther down the main hall toward the back of the school and the science department. It was the farthest distance from the front of the school and Dr. Delmar said it was always a good idea to have a stack of papers in that area for students and teachers who spent most of their time there each day.

He was placing a stack of papers in the rack in that section of the building when he heard someone come through the double doors at the back of the building – the same doors Kaiah went through every day with her marching band instruments. He straightened up and looked toward the door and noticed that it was Mr. Boreland … and Sam was walking with him. The two seemed to be arguing. Chet was standing on the opposite side of the hallway in a somewhat recessed area that was slightly shadowed, and they didn't seem to notice him.

"I told you, I don't have time to take care of it today!" Mr. Boreland said with a growl in his voice. "You'll have to make sure that loud-mouthed rooster is fed and watered today."

"I don't have time to take care of it, either!" Sam retorted. "I don't know why I always have to be the one to do it, anyway! You're the one who decided to move that chicken."

Mr. Boreland stopped suddenly and turned to face Sam. He leaned close, and Sam flinched back.

"Yes, but it's your fault we have so many clucking chickens in the first place," Mr. Boreland hissed. "I told you we could have one – just one – and now they're multiplying like crazy!"

Chet frowned in confusion as he tried to understand

what they were talking about. As the primary biology teacher at the high school, it wasn't unusual for Mr. Boreland to have various animals for his lessons. Chet's own science class was supposed to start a unit on amphibians in coming weeks, and they'd been informed that they would be dissecting frogs and learning to care for turtles. Chet had also heard of other classes dissecting things like baby pigs and cats, and still more classes were responsible for caring for rodents or bunnies. He hadn't heard of any of the science teachers bringing in chickens, though. But as he thought about it, he decided it could make sense considering the school mascot was the chicken hawk. And from a scientific standpoint, chickens would provide students the opportunity to learn about eggs and reproduction and things like that. Still … it didn't make sense that Mr. Boreland would be so mad about it, nor that he would entrust Sam, of all people, with the responsibility of caring for those animals. Maybe it was a responsibility that came with senior-level classes.

"I told you, it's not my fault!" Sam said, standing up straighter and glaring at the teacher. "My Dad was the one who – "

At that moment Sam looked in the direction of Chet and noticed him standing there by the newspaper rack. A look of panic crossed his face, and Mr. Boreland turned toward Chet immediately. Chet flinched back at the look on Mr. Boreland's face.

"What are you doing here?!" Mr. Boreland demanded.

"P-p-putting the newspapers in the rack, sir," Chet replied nervously. "We d-do it every F-Friday morning."

Mr. Boreland blinked and frowned, then looked at Sam questioningly. Sam had recovered from his shock and was now glaring daggers at Chet. He sighed heavily and glanced at Mr. Boreland, nodding to affirm what Chet had just said.

"It's true," Sam said. "I forgot about it because I haven't had to do it for the past three years."

Mr. Boreland looked back at Chet and frowned more deeply.

"Well, get on with it then!" he said. "And stop eavesdropping on other people's conversations."

Chet gulped and nodded emphatically. He settled the stack of papers into the rack and then hurriedly wheeled the dolly toward the back doors. His next stop was the newspaper rack that sat beside the entrance to the football stadium. That's where the majority of the papers would go, in preparation for the Homecoming game that evening. They'd printed a thousand extra papers this week in the expectation that the football game would draw a larger-than-average crowd. He looked over his shoulder as he pushed the dolly through the doors and saw both Sam and Mr. Boreland glaring at him. He hurried out as quickly as he could.

He tried to shake off the encounter he'd just had as he wheeled the dolly along the pathway toward the football stadium. In the distance he could see more cars arriving at the school – some of them parking in spaces allotted to students and some of them pulling up to the front of the school and dropping students off. Chet quickened his pace. He still had to put the remaining papers in the rack by the stadium, return the dolly to the newspaper office and then make it to his class on time.

He couldn't help dwelling on the interaction he'd just witnessed between Sam and Mr. Boreland. He ran the conversation through his mind multiple times, so engrossed in his thoughts that he barely paid attention to what he was doing when stacking the newspapers in the rack. Something was off about the conversation, but Chet couldn't quite put his finger on it. It wasn't unusual for upperclassmen to be given special assignments by teachers, so it wasn't out of the ordinary for Sam to be having a private conversation with a teacher before school started. What bugged Chet about it was how angry Mr. Boreland had seemed. Chet had seen teachers be frustrated with students before, but never outright hostile. It had almost seemed as if Mr. Boreland had wanted to take a swing at Sam. And what had Sam been about to say about his father? How did that have anything to do with taking care of a chicken … or chickens multiplying … or where those chickens were being kept?

Chet was so consumed with his thoughts that he didn't notice Jess standing in front of him until he almost ran her over with the dolly. She was holding out her phone toward him, and he could see his article in the Scribbler glaring out at him from the mobile website.

"What is this?!" She demanded. "Why did you write this?! I told you he didn't run away! His mom says he didn't run away! So why would you write something that clearly tells people that he ran away?!"

Chet flinched back at her barrage of accusations and tried to compose himself as he thought of an appropriate response.

"I know …" Chet began. "It's … complicated."

"Complicated?!" Jess retorted, her face turning red as she glared at him. "How is it complicated?!"

"I … well … there's just not a lot of evidence, Jess," Chet said lamely. "What am I supposed to write? Nobody knows anything!"

Jess snorted and glared at him more deeply.

"*I* know that he hasn't answered his phone in two weeks," she said. "*I* know that we've been best friends for six years and we've barely gone a day without talking with each other, and he'd never just leave without letting me know. *I* know that he feels responsible for taking care of his mom and he'd never just leave her like this. *I* know that something bad has happened to him and no one else but me and his mom seems to care! And now this article is just gonna convince people to stop looking for him."

Chet shrugged uncomfortably and tried to regain his composure.

"I don't think my article has that much power," he said. "I mean, just because I write an article for The Scribbler doesn't mean the police are going to stop looking for him. They can't. It's a missing person's report. They have to keep looking until they find him."

"Yeah, well, they sure aren't trying very hard," Jess said, lowering her phone to her side and sagging like a balloon that has just had its air let out. "They've basically given up, and this article is basically saying that's alright – that we all should give up because obviously Gavin has run away. Well, it's not obvious to me! What *is* obvious to me is that someone has done something to him, and he needs help!"

Chet looked with pity on Jess as she folded her arms in frustration. He didn't blame her for being upset – if Chunk had gone missing like this, he'd have been frantic to find his best friend, too. And he certainly wouldn't have given up looking just because a few people suggested that he might have run away. So it was perfectly understandable that Jess would be at the end of her rope like this. But Chet had no idea what to do to help her.

"What do you want me to do, Jess?" Chet said in exasperation. "I have an editor who hates me and changes half of what I write. The police won't tell me anything more than what's in that article. Gavin's mom is a wreck and half-drunk every time we talk to her. His dad is even worse. And there's literally no one else who has any kind of information about him. So what am I supposed to do?"

"Don't give up!" She retorted immediately, unfolding her arms and learning toward him. "You're the only one trying to figure this all out. Everybody else is giving up, but you don't have to! You can keep digging."

Chet was taken aback by her faith in his abilities as an investigative reporter. A kernel of something began to ignite in his chest as he considered what she was challenging him with. He'd spent the last two years trying to figure out what had happened to his father, and that mystery was no nearer to being resolved than it had been when he'd started. He couldn't seem to solve that mystery, but maybe if he kept trying he'd be able to figure out this one. His father had never given up on a story – it was one of the things he most admired about his dad. It was the main reason why he wanted to be an investigative reporter himself. And as Jess stood there in front of him, challenging him to live up to that purpose, he felt that spark of resolve in his chest fan into a flame. He set his jaw, straightened his back and adopted a look of determination.

"You're right," he said to Jess. "Somebody has to figure this out. I won't give up. But I need your help. Can you meet tonight after the game with me and Kaiah and we can compare notes? Maybe you've noticed something we've missed."

Jess gave him a tentative smile and nodded with relief.

"Yes," she said. "I'll wait for you just outside the entrance."

Chet nodded in reply and the two parted ways – Jess to go to her class and Chet to return the dolly to the newspaper room. As he reentered the building, he noticed that the hallways were starting to fill up with students hurrying to their classes. He knew he only had a few minutes to put the dolly away and gather his things for his first class. He was just about to push the dolly into the newspaper room when he noticed there were three people already there – Sam, Caleb and Jim. The interaction with Sam from just a few minutes earlier was still fresh, and he didn't want to have another confrontation with his editor. So, he pulled up short and lingered by the doorway, leaning in to eavesdrop on their conversation.

"So how much are we gonna make?" Caleb asked, his eyes gleaming as he beamed up at Sam in expectation.

"I dunno," Sam said, brushing him off. "A lot … if you do your job."

Caleb frowned.

"Of course I'll do my job," Caleb said. "It's not that difficult. Me and Jim just have to go around collecting from everyone. You're the one who has to do your job."

"I told you, it's taken care of," Sam said. "Aaron has already agreed to it."

"You sure?" Caleb asked. "He could ruin everything, you know. It is Homecoming, after all."

"He won't ruin anything," Sam said confidently, a sly smirk crossing his face. "He knows too much and he knows that I'll spill the beans if he doesn't play along. He's too worried about losing a scholarship to back out now."

"Sam … I'm not sure about all this," Jim said.

Sam stood up suddenly and towered over Jim, glaring down at him in anger.

"Just do what you're supposed to do and it'll be over tonight," Sam said. "And keep your mouth shut! Nobody else can know about this. Too many people know already."

Jim shrank back and swallowed, then nodded slightly. He and Caleb both seemed cowed by Sam. The conversation seemed to be at an end, however, as they all gathered their backpacks and turned toward the door to leave. Chet jumped and then decided at the last minute that the least suspicious thing he could do would be to just push the dolly into the room as if he hadn't heard anything. So that's what he did, all the while keeping his eyes down and trying as best he could to look like everything was normal.

"Well hello there, Lord Chetfield," Caleb said bitingly. "You couldn't order any of your subjects to distribute the papers for you, eh? What do you call yourselves? The News Hawks? What a stupid name."

Jim and Sam both joined Caleb as he laughed at Chet's expense. He did his best to ignore them as he pushed the dolly into corner right next to the file cabinet. Then he grabbed his backpack from the chair where he'd left it and brushed past the boys and out of the room. He noticed out of the corner of his eye that Sam was frowning at him with a note of worry on his face, but none of them said anything more to him as he rushed out of the room.

It was a short walk to his first class – Math, his least favorite subject. His head was swirling with all that he'd experienced over the past half hour – from Mr. Boreland and Sam, to his confrontation with Jess, and the strange conversation he'd overheard with Caleb and Jim. What were the three of them up to? Why was Mr. Boreland so angry about a chicken? And how was he going to solve the mystery of the missing mascot?

CHS Enters Homecoming Game As Favorites Over Rival PHS

By Caleb Fletcher
The Scribbler · Sports Reporter

CHETFIELD, OH – A long-standing rivalry between Chetfield High School (CHS) and Pickering High School (PHS) takes center stage this Friday night as the two state-championship-contending football teams clash in an early season battle.

CHS enters the game as the odds-on favorites, thanks to recent disciplinary action from Pickering school administrators that led to the suspension of five of their team's starters. Though the teams enter the game fairly evenly matched – pre-season predictions had Pickering as the favorite to win the state championship – the loss of five of their starters has tipped the scales in favor of the home team.

"You always want to win a game any way you can, and we're happy to face a quality team like Pickering when they're in a weakened position," said CHS head coach Irv Smith. "I feel good about our chances to come out of this game with a victory, which would put us in the lead in the championship hunt. This could be a good year for Chetfield."

Coach Smith's confidence seems to have bled over onto his players, as many of them expressed positive attitudes this week in the days leading up to the tilt against Pickering.

"We're going to crush them," said CHS quarterback Aaron Johnson. "They don't have a chance."

Much of CHS's offensive strategy revolves around its rushing attack. Touted as one of the best rushing quarterbacks in Ohio high school football, Johnson is known for his ability to scramble out of the pocket and create plays with his feet. Though there has been some criticism of his accuracy passing the ball, he wreaks havoc against opposing defenses when he can scramble and pick up chunks of yardage on the run. He led the team in rushing last year, but has worked hard on his passing game during the off-season and is promising better things to come with the offense this season.

"I feel great about our chances not only to win this week, but to go all the way to the state championship," Johnson said. "We're all clicking and grooving together perfectly. That title trophy is basically ours already."

The Homecoming game against Pickering begins at 7 p.m. on Friday. Those planning to attend the game are encouraged to arrive early, as a large contingency of Pickering fans are expected to attend the game, as well.

CHAPTER 9

AWKWARD MOMENTS

het looked up from his phone and across the football field at the stands on the opposite side. Caleb's story in The Scribbler had been accurate in that quite a large contingent of fans from Pickering had made the drive down to Chetfield to attend the game. The visiting team's bleachers were packed so full that Pickering fans had been forced to spread out in a wide fan along the sidelines. Hundreds of people surrounded the field, standing just beyond the end zones on both ends. Between the Chetfield fans and the Pickering fans there were easily 5,000 people attending the game.

Chet sat in the home-team stands about halfway up on the left side. Next to him sat Noélle and her family – a younger brother named Nathan, twin younger sisters and her parents. His own mother and sister, Chloe, sat on his other side. He felt a bit claustrophobic sandwiched between everyone like that, especially with so many other people pressing in on him from behind and in front. He tried to ignore the feeling, however, and focus on the game. It was difficult, though, as he didn't really care about football and his mind was still swimming with his various encounters from earlier that morning. He hadn't had a chance to talk with Kaiah about anything yet, and when he'd shared his experiences with Noélle as they sat there in the stands, her response had been noncommittal. He liked Noélle and her confidence, but she was sometimes frustrating in her lack of ambition and drive. She wasn't like Kaiah, who shared his passion for getting to the bottom of things and fighting for the truth. He needed to bounce some ideas off Kaiah and see if she could provide a fresh perspective to what he'd seen and heard that morning.

It was nearing halftime and so far the game had been pretty evenly matched. The teams were tied at 17 points apiece, with Pickering having just evened the score on a long 40-yard breakaway run from their running back, who was easily the best player on their team. Chet looked down at the CHS sideline and saw Aaron Johnson talking very animatedly to some of the other players on the team. Chunk was sitting on the bench looking up at Aaron, absorbing whatever it was the senior captain of the team was spouting. Aaron wasn't having a very good game so far – he'd thrown two interceptions and fumbled the ball in what had appeared to be a botched snap. Chet wasn't sure who had been at fault

– Aaron or Chunk – but Coach Smith had seemed to blame the latter as he'd yelled at Chunk so loudly after the play that Chet had been able to hear it over the din of the crowd from where he was sitting. He felt bad for his friend, and knew that Chunk was probably stewing inside.

Chet was distracted by some motion off to the right of the field, and when he looked in that direction he noticed the marching band approaching the field from the rear of the school. He glanced at the game clock and saw that there were only five minutes left before halftime. CHS was lining up to receive the kickoff from Pickering following their most recent score, and Chet wondered if they'd be able to score again before halftime. Pickering's defense was playing very well.

Chet looked again at the marching band and decided on a whim to walk down there and see if he could say hi to Kaiah before she took the field for the halftime show. They'd had a rough week, following the incident in study hall on Tuesday, and she hadn't really said much to him since. It was obvious she was hurt and jealous about Emily, even though Chet didn't really think there should be anything to be jealous about. But he did feel bad about the uncomfortable vibes between the two of them, and he hoped maybe wishing her luck might be an olive branch he could extend.

"Hey, I'm gonna go see if I can find Kaiah and wish her luck," Chet said to Noélle, standing up and laying a hand on his mom's shoulder to get her attention and let her know he wanted to shuffle down the row. His mom blinked at him, then smiled and moved her knees out of the way so Chet could get by. He could hear Noélle's twittering laughter behind him, but he chose to ignore it.

As he climbed down the stairs, he started thinking about the lack of information they'd been able to gather over the course of the week. He'd felt confident they were onto something when they'd compared notes in study hall on Tuesday, but in the three days since then they hadn't been able to take any steps forward. Chunk hadn't gotten anywhere with Aaron – though Chet doubted he had tried very hard. Not that he could blame him. Chet hadn't tried very hard to get an interview with Sam's dad, either. For some reason the editor of The Scribbler did not like Chet very much, and Chet didn't look forward to a confrontation with the older boy just in the hopes of getting an interview that Sam probably wouldn't allow to be run in the newspaper anyway. Kaiah also hadn't tried very hard to get Mr. Boreland to talk, stating that when she'd lingered after class on Wednesday he'd given her such a discouraging look that she left the classroom in a rush without saying anything. Noélle was the only one to have contributed anything, letting them know that Aaron's girlfriend, Abby, had suggested that Caleb and Jim – the two sports reporters for The Scribbler – were taking bets from other students on the Homecoming game. Chet wasn't sure that meant anything, but he had told the News Hawks to follow the money, so he supposed he should give it some consideration. But in the two weeks since school had started, Chet had begun to consider Caleb and Jim as relatively unintelligent. If they were involved in Gavin's disappearance, or had knowledge of anything related to it, Chet didn't think they were smart enough to keep their mouths shut and not let something slip. Essentially, in his opinion, their sheer stupidity exonerated them.

Once Chet was in the open area behind the stands his way was basically clear, as most people were still in their seats watching the game. There was the odd person here and there hurrying back from the bathroom or the concession stand, but for the most part the walkway was empty. Because of that he was able to make his way relatively quickly around the field to where the band was gathering. He glanced at the game clock again and realized only a minute of game time had passed, meaning there were still four minutes on the clock. When he looked at the band, he saw Kaiah and the auxiliary team standing off to the side. Most of the instruments were loaded onto a trailer that was connected to a four-wheeler. Kaiah was standing toward the back of the trailer, looking over her shoulder toward the school with a worried expression on her face. Chet set his shoulders and took a deep breath, then walked over to her.

"Hey Kaiah," he said loudly so that she'd hear him over the roar of the crowd. He must have yelled a little too loudly, however, as she jumped nearly a foot off the ground and landed facing him with her hands up in a defensive stance. When she saw it was him, she put a hand to her chest and breathed out heavily.

"Sheesh Chet! You scared me to death!" she said, frowning at him as she looked over his shoulder as if searching for something.

"Why are you so jumpy?" Chet said with a smile. "Are you nervous about the halftime performance? You're gonna be great!"

Kaiah stopped searching over his shoulder to give him a look of suspicion, then returned to her perusal of the crowd behind him. She was searching so thoroughly that Chet looked over his shoulder, as well, trying to see what she was looking for.

"I *am* nervous," Kaiah said, "but that's not why I'm jumpy."

Chet turned back to her and gave her a questioning look. "What's going on?" he said. "You seem very worried about something."

Kaiah looked at him again and this time her gaze lingered.

"Before the game started I saw Caleb, Jim, and Sam in the back hall talking to Aaron Johnson," Kaiah said. "He didn't seem very happy, and neither did Sam. They were yelling at each other, and Sam said something like, 'You made promises, Aaron. You can't back out now.' I couldn't really figure out what they were talking about. But the problem is that they all saw me – Sam and Caleb and Jim, I mean. They saw me watching them … and they did not look happy."

Chet frowned in thought and wondered what it was

Kaiah had stumbled upon with the four boys. After the altercation at the poker game, Chet thought it unusual that Sam and Aaron would want to talk to each other, but it sounded like they had some kind of agreement or something. He could understand why Kaiah might be nervous about the boys, though. He was about to tell her as much when someone suddenly tapped him on the shoulder.

"Hey, Chet, I thought that was you!" a girl's voice said, and when Chet turned to look, he recognized Emily from Pickering. She was wearing essentially the same outfit as the last time he'd seen her, though now she had a blue rhino painted on her cheek – the PHS mascot. It made her look even cuter, and he couldn't help but feel a flush creep up his cheeks.

"Uh … hi Emily," Chet said, sparing a quick glance at Kaiah, who was frowning at him. She crossed her arms and adopted a posture that was obviously not happy. "Enjoying the game?"

"Yes!" Emily said. "I was worried we'd get crushed, but it's actually a pretty even match-up. I think we might have a chance of beating you guys, in fact."

She punched him playfully in the arm, and Chet chuckled. Kaiah cleared her throat dramatically, and when Chet looked at her, she was tapping her foot and staring at him with such an intent glare that he flinched back.

"Uh … Emily … this is my friend Kaiah," Chet said, gesturing to her. "Kaiah, this is Emily. She's one of the reporters for the Pickering newspaper."

Emily turned to Kaiah and stuck out her hand, bestowing her with a broad smile. Kaiah seemed taken aback for a minute, then returned the smile and stuck out her hand, as well – shaking Emily's hand firmly. Chet knew Kaiah well enough by now to recognize the frostiness behind her smile, but Emily didn't seem to notice.

"Kaiah's on The Scribbler staff with me," Chet said to Emily. "We've been working on the Gavin story together – you know, the missing student."

Emily turned back to him and smiled again.

"Yes, I've been keeping up on it," she said. "When you solve the mystery, do you think you'd be willing to share your notes with me? I'd love to follow up on our end of it, considering the whole prank thing and all."

Chet nodded slowly and unconsciously raised a hand to his eye. There was barely a bruise left. If someone wasn't looking closely, they'd never know he'd had a massive black eye a week earlier. Emily smiled at him again.

"Great!" she said. "Thanks! Oh – by the way. I wanted to ask you: Do you know why your editor would be meeting with our newspaper adviser?"

Chet tilted his head and couldn't keep the confused look from his face. He looked at Kaiah, who seemed equally baffled. She shrugged her shoulders as if to say, *"Your guess is as good as mine."*

"No …" Chet said. "Why?"

"Well, he was at our school yesterday, and that's not the first time I've seen him there," Emily said. "He always meets with our newspaper adviser in his office, then goes somewhere else in the school – I don't know where – before leaving. I didn't think really anything about it the first time other than wondering if it had to do with some regional journalism thing or something. But now that it's happened three times it seems a little weird to me."

Chet frowned again, but Kaiah stepped forward and had a pondering look on her face.

"Is your adviser into sports?" she asked.

"Yes!" Emily said emphatically. "It's, like, all he talks about. He always wants us to put sports news on the front page and he has a TV in his office so he can watch games whenever he wants. That's him right over there."

She pointed to a group of Pickering fans a few feet away, and when Chet realized who she was pointing at, he flinched in shock.

"Kaiah! That's the guy," he said emphatically. "The guy Mr. Boreland was meeting with at the Pickering game!"

Kaiah shared a shocked look with him, then her eyes got a vacant look and he could tell she was thinking of something.

"Who's Mr. Boreland?" Emily asked curiously, looking back and forth at them as she tried to understand why they seemed so shocked. "What does our adviser liking sports have to do with anything?"

Kaiah didn't answer her but instead turned to Chet with a suddenly excited look on her face. She grabbed his arm and shook it.

"Chet, I think I've figured it out!" She said. "I think –"

"Kaiah, get your butt in line! We're about to go!"

The voice of the band teacher rang out over Kaiah's head and made her jump. She turned quickly and Chet looked toward the field, noticing that the clock was winding down its last seconds toward halftime. The game was still tied at 17 points apiece, and already the teams were starting to jog off the field. Kaiah turned back to Chet quickly and gave him a desperate look.

"Find me after the show," she said in a rush. "I think I've got it figured out. And stay away from Sam and Mr. Boreland!"

Before Chet could respond she was moving away to join the team. Why did she want him to stay away from Sam and Mr. Boreland? That was the opposite of what he wanted to do. How was he going to solve the mystery if he didn't figure out what they were up to? But Kaiah couldn't answer any of those questions at the moment. She jumped onto the trailer mere seconds before the four-wheeler took off, driving the instruments to the edge of the field.

"Is she your girlfriend or something?" Emily asked

suddenly, making him draw back in shock.

"What?! No! I mean … no!" Chet said, obviously flustered.

"Oh …" she said, a slow smile creeping onto her face. "… good."

Chet's face turned red in a flash, and he had to look away so she wouldn't notice. He was pretty sure she saw it anyway, but he tried to ignore her standing there beside him. He stared directly ahead at the band and didn't look at her, even when he heard her laugh lightly beside him. She took a step closer to him, her shoulder brushing his just slightly. He felt a flush of excitement but didn't have the first idea what to do. The fingers on her right hand were so close to his own that they whispered against his skin and sent a chill of delight along his body. He didn't move – just kept watching the field as the marching band started its performance.

About halfway through the show Chet's gaze started to wander and he looked at the people in the stands and along the edge of the field. Easily half of the people in attendance weren't paying attention to the band and had instead opted to use halftime as a chance to stretch their legs, use the restroom, or get a snack from the concession stand. People were moving around all over the place, and Chet was again impressed by how many people were in attendance.

Suddenly he noticed red-haired Caleb standing off to the side, not far away from where he and Emily were standing. He was talking with a teacher – Mr. Clark, the world history teacher. The older man didn't seem happy at whatever it was Caleb was saying to him. As Chet watched, the teacher sighed and reached into his pocket, pulling out his wallet. He pulled some cash out of the wallet and then handed it to Caleb. Chet's eyebrows rose nearly to the top of his forehead in surprise. As Caleb started to turn away, Mr. Clark grabbed his shoulder and said something to him. Caleb seemed surprised for a minute, then gave the teacher a wicked smile and pulled a notepad out of his back pocket, wrote something down and then turned and walked away.

"I have to go," Chet said dismissively to Emily, deciding in that moment to follow Caleb and figure out what it was he was doing. "Sorry."

Emily seemed surprised and disappointed, but she nodded at him as he walked away, and a moment later he saw her walking toward a group of PHS students. She was a pretty girl, and if she really did like him as much as it seemed she did, then he felt great! But he wasn't sure how he felt about Kaiah, and besides, Emily was a student at a completely different school. And on top of all that, his mom wouldn't let him have a girlfriend until he was 16 anyway, which was another year-and-a-half from now.

She is pretty, though, he thought to himself as he started tailing Caleb.

The older red-haired boy made his way through the crowd around to the wide walkway behind the bleachers. The band's performance sounded muffled as the noise was blocked by the stands, but Chet could tell that it was reaching its climax. He took a quick look at the time on his phone and noted that halftime would be over in about five more minutes.

He followed Caleb up to the concession stand and hung back as the older boy purchased a candy bar. Chet wondered if he used the money he'd just received from Mr. Clark. Another boy Chet didn't know walked up to Caleb and started talking with him. Caleb drew him to the side, slightly behind the concession stand and out of the way of the other people milling around. Chet had to move closer so he could see what was happening. He walked all the way up to the concession stand. Caleb looked over his shoulder at that exact moment and looked directly at Chet. Panicking, Chet looked away immediately and noticed a stack of Chetfield Daily newspapers on the corner of the concession stand. He grabbed one quickly and pretended to start reading.

Old Chetfield Water Plant Scheduled For Demolition This Friday

By Susan Watergarden
Chetfield Daily News · City Government Correspondent

CHETFIELD, OH – Chetfield will say goodbye to one of its oldest pieces of history this Friday evening when the original Chetfield Water Plant building is demolished.

The water treatment works was constructed adjacent to Chetfield Reservoir in 1917. At the time, the city chose to employ the services of architect Alsbet Samuelson, who was well-known around the world for his elegant and extravagant designs. Hailing from Norway, this young architect designed a waterworks that would incorporate a labyrinthine style that featured many halls and rooms that became known throughout the region as the "water maze." Employees of the water works have shared stories of getting lost in the halls of the water maze many times over the years. Though it became an endearing quality of the facility, it also was one of the features that led the company to shut it down and build a newer, more updated facility in 1982.

The city has continued to own the property upon which the old building has sat, but earlier this year the city council voted to allow the sale of the property. Approximately 22 acres, including the building, were purchased last month by the Logeberg Company – a Belgium-based business that manufactures bearings for engines.

"We're excited to welcome the Logeberg Company to our city," said Chetfield Mayor Ryan Robinson. "Their new facility will bring hundreds of new jobs to our community and will be a boost to the economy. We're looking forward to a long and amicable relationship with our new friends from Belgium."

A spokesperson for the Logeberg Company said the demolition of the old water plant is necessary, as its interior is not suited for the kind of manufacturing facility the company needs, and a renovation of the building would cost more than it would to bulldoze everything and construct a brand new building.

The company has opted to hire the professional demolition team CV Demo from Cincinnati for the job. According to CV owner Chad Brancofski, the process of destroying the old building begins with an explosion.

"We'll rig the entire building with explosives that upon detonation will cause the building to cave in on itself, essentially," Brancofski said. "From there we can haul away the rubble and recycle any of the leftover metal."

Brancofski said the explosion is slated for Friday evening following the Chetfield High School Homecoming game. He said anyone wishing to watch should gather on the CHS baseball field.

CHAPTER 10

PLACE YOUR BETS

het glanced up at Caleb and the other boy as he finished reading the article on the front page of the Chetfield Daily News. A picture of the old water plant filled the top half of the paper, but Chet barely paid attention. He was trying to be discreet while watching what Caleb was doing. He heard the crowd roar behind him and figured the second half must have started. The other boy with Caleb must have realized the same thing because he looked longingly toward the stands. Then he nodded in agreement to whatever it was Caleb had been trying to convince him of and hurriedly reached into his pocket to pull out some money, which he handed over to Caleb before running away toward the stands.

Caleb smiled triumphantly to himself, then turned and

started walking down the path behind the stands. Chet waited long enough not to be suspicious, then started to follow. He tried to focus on keeping Caleb in front of him, but a rush of people who had also heard the roar of the crowd ran past him trying to hurry back to their seats. He was jostled momentarily and had to take his eyes off Caleb. When he was able to steady himself and look again, Caleb was gone.

Chet stopped and looked in every direction, searching desperately for the boy. With his red hair, he shouldn't have been hard to find. Chet rushed forward and ran around the bend, looking in every direction. When he got to the end of the stands he stopped and spun in frustration. That's when he caught sight of Caleb and another boy – yet another student Chet didn't know – standing in an alcove a few paces off. It was dark toward this end of the walkway, and the alcove was hidden in shadow, so it was no wonder Chet had run past without seeing them. It didn't look like Caleb or the other boy had noticed him, however, so he walked to the wall as nonchalantly as he could and tried to watch what they were doing.

As before, Caleb exchanged money with the other boy, pocketed the cash and then walked off in the same direction he'd just come. The other boy, however, walked in Chet's direction, obviously headed to the ramp and his seat in the stands. He was nearly on top of Chet when he noticed him leaning against the wall, and he flinched when he saw Chet staring at him. Chet could only describe the look on the boy's face as one of guilt and panic, which was quickly masked with anger and a scowl. But the two didn't exchange any words, and the other boy continued on his way. Chet watched him round the corner to the ramp, then leaped away from the wall and hurried after Caleb.

A collective groan suddenly came from the home team stands, with a counter-point cheer from the visiting team stands a moment later. Chet assumed something bad had happened for his school's team, but he wasn't going to rush up the next ramp to find out. Caleb did, though, turning quickly and running the few steps up the ramp to get a view of the field. Chet stopped at the corner and watched Caleb stand at the railing for a few moments, watching the game without taking a seat.

"What happened?!" a man's voice asked from behind Chet, startling him and causing him to jump. Chet shook his head as the man looked at him with expectation.

"I dunno," Chet said. "I didn't see."

The man frowned, then made his way up the ramp. Caleb must have heard the man's footsteps because he glanced over his shoulder, and Chet ducked back behind the corner. He hoped Caleb hadn't seen him. He made a slow count of 30 before peeking back around the corner, and he saw that Caleb was once again watching the game while leaning on the railing.

The two of them stayed that way for the rest of the third quarter – Caleb leaning on the railing and Chet leaning against the wall, peeking around the corner up the ramp at him. The game continued to go back and forth between the two teams, and Chet kept up with what was happening by listening to the occasional announcements over the loud-speakers. The first groan from the crowd that had prompted Caleb to walk up the ramp had been because of another turnover by CHS. Pickering took advantage of that turnover and turned it into a score, gaining the lead 24-17. Chetfield responded on the next drive, however, by earning a touchdown of their own and tying the score. The crowd went crazy at that, and some grit fell on Chet's head from above when fans in the stands started stomping their feet.

Pickering was able to score again in the moments before the end of the third quarter, giving them the lead going into the fourth quarter. In the last seconds before the quarter officially ended, people started trickling down the ramp to get a head-start on the bathrooms. Caleb also seemed inclined to beat the crowd, as he turned away from the railing and made his way back down the ramp. Chet ducked out of the way and then did his best to mingle in the crowd as Caleb walked by. Thankfully, the older boy didn't seem to notice him.

Chet again followed Caleb along the walkway and watched as he interacted with two more students he didn't recognize. Each time the same thing happened – the other boy handed over cash to Caleb, who stuffed it in his pocket, gave them a sneer, and then walked off. The game re-started, but Caleb seemed more concerned with getting money from people than he did with watching the game. A little farther on he stopped and chatted with a teacher, who also gave him money. Chet couldn't believe what he was seeing.

By the time Chet had followed Caleb to the other end of the bleachers and down the path that led to the edge of the field, the fourth-quarter clock showed only six minutes left. Caleb stopped at the edge of the field where the railing ended and leaned against it to watch the rest of the game. Chet stopped abruptly and emulated him, leaning casually against the railing as if that had been his intention from the beginning. Still, Caleb didn't seem to notice that he was following.

Chet couldn't help but be drawn into the conclusion of the game as he stood there. The last five minutes of the game were intense, and the buzz of the crowd created an excitement that seemed to make the air sizzle. Chetfield had scored early in the fourth quarter to again tie the score at 31-31. Both defenses held their opponents scoreless on their ensuing drives, and with four minutes left on the clock Chetfield had the ball and was driving down the field.

Aaron looked like he'd shaken off whatever jitters he had from earlier in the game because he was single-handedly willing the team to win. He started the drive by launching a 15-yard strike to one of the receivers for an immediate first down. Two plays later it looked like he was going to be sacked, but he somehow escaped and slipped along the left sideline for a 12-yard scramble and another first down. He threw for seven yards and 13 yards, successively, on the next two plays and had the team well into the Pickering end of the field. Chet heard someone nearby tell the person next to them that if Chetfield could get another 20 yards they'd be in easy field goal range and could seal the game.

Chet took a quick look toward Caleb to make sure he was still there – which he was – and then turned back to the game. There was less than two minutes on the clock now, and as Aaron tucked the ball and took off running down the field again, the seconds ticked down. He gained about 15 of the 20 yards to get them into field goal position, leaving them about five yards short. Coach Smith called a time out and Chet looked at the clock. It read 1:27.

Chet looked at the offensive line and squinted to see if he could make out Chunk. He found his friend easily enough, but the distance was too great for him to make out Chunk's face from behind his face mask. He could tell his friend was winded, however, because he stood there with hands on hips, his shoulders moving up and down as he gulped deep breaths. A team manager – it looked like Jess – walked up to him and held up a water bottle. Chunk nodded and Jess squirted water into his mouth.

Seeing Jess reminded Chet of Principal Miller's promise that Charlie the Chicken hawk would be replaced by a real live chicken. Chet began searching the sidelines, and sure enough there was a rooster being paraded along the sidelines by the cheer leading squad. Chet again wondered why Mr. Boreland had been so angry with Sam about the chicken.

His musing was interrupted by one of the refs blowing a

whistle. The timeout was over and the teams were lining up to start again. Chet watched as Chunk snapped the ball and Aaron took five steps back, arm cocked and looking down field for an open receiver. Chet was surprised that Coach Smith would call a passing play considering they only needed five yards to get into field goal range, but he also didn't know football that well and he assumed the coach knew what he was doing.

Aaron planted his feet and reached back his arm, then slung forward and released the ball. Chet could tell from the moment it left Aaron's hands that it was a bad pass. Though Aaron was untouched when he threw the ball, it left his hand in a tumbling end-over-end wobble. And instead of zipping into the hands of an open receiver, it flipped and flopped its way into the arms of a defender, who gathered the ball into his belly and ran the other direction for 40 yards before someone from the Chetfield team could tackle him. The cheers from the Pickering side of the stadium were overpowering in the face of the silence from the Chetfield fans.

Chet stayed where he was and watched as three plays later Pickering's running back was able to break a tackle and rush his way into the end zone. There were 17 seconds left on the clock as the Rhinos kicked through the extra point and took the lead 38-31. Chetfield was unable to use that time to do anything even remotely close to scoring.

Chet looked toward Caleb as the stands began to empty. Chetfield fans grumbled and glared at the Pickering fans who were cheering and chanting and mobbing the field. Caleb turned away from the railing and toward the path that led to the locker rooms. Chet noticed a grin on the boy's face, and he wondered why Caleb – the school's primary sports reporter – would be happy about his team losing such an important game. Chet felt fairly certain this dashed all hopes of CHS contending for a state championship.

Caleb started walking quickly toward the locker rooms, and Chet hurried to keep up. Instead of stopping at the locker rooms, however, Caleb continued past the building toward the back of the school and the double doors that led to the hall Kaiah used to bring the auxiliary equipment to the field. Caleb didn't even hesitate in going through the doors, and after waiting long enough for Caleb to have moved well beyond the doors, Chet followed.

Caleb wasn't in the hall when Chet walked through the doors, but he heard voices just around the corner. Chet moved toward the voices and realized they were coming from the science labs.

Chet eased his way around the corner and peeked through the door into one of the science labs. Caleb was talking with Jim, and they both seemed very happy. Jim pulled a wad of cash out of his pocket and handed it to Caleb, who pulled even more money out of his own pocket. Combined, it looked like *a lot* of money. Chet wondered what he should do next – whether he should try to find another teacher or someone like Principal Miller – when a hand suddenly clamped down on his shoulder.

"Well hello there, Lord Chetfield," a voice said beside him, making him jump. Chet tried to run away, but the hand on his shoulder held him down while another hand grabbed his arm and twisted it up at a painful angle. Chet turned his head and looked into the eyes of his editor. "Eavesdropping again, are we?"

Sam smiled wickedly at Chet, then pushed him forward into the science lab. He kicked the door closed behind him as Caleb and Jim looked up at the commotion.

Pickering Pulls Off Upset Win Over Chetfield In Massive Homecoming Battle

By Sam Chapin
The Scribbler · Editor-In-Chief

CHETFIELD, OH – An upset that will be talked about for years took place Friday night under the lights at Chetfield High School stadium as visiting Pickering pulled off a late-game victory over the heavily favored Chickenhawks.

Pickering was without five of its starters due to disciplinary action from school officials following a prank against Chetfield that resulted in the injury of a CHS student. As such, the pre-game predictions had Pickering flagging as the underdogs, despite preseason rankings that had them first in the state and the odds-on favorites to take this year's championship. But five turnovers from Chetfield's star quarterback Aaron Johnson led to three scores on Pickering's side and proved too much for the home team to overcome.

Pickering was led by running back Joshua Davis, who racked up 220 total yards of offense on his own, as well as three of the team's five touchdowns. He capped the night with a 30-yard scamper in the final minute of the game, eluding tackles on his way for the score that would eventually put Chetfield away. His athletic prowess was put on full display with that single run and showcased why he is one of the top Division 1 recruits in the state. Pickering was also led by junior quarterback Dan Taylor, who threw for 172 yards and one touchdown. Tight end Evan Stephens caught that touchdown, a corner-of-the-end-zone fade that was perfectly placed by Taylor so that Stephens could use his height to go up for the ball over the top of the shorter defenders. The other touchdown for Pickering was put on the board by the team's defense following a fumble by Johnson early in the third quarter.

Despite his miscues, Johnson had a good night statistically, accounting for 160 yards rushing and three touchdowns. He also threw the ball for an additional 182 yards and one passing touchdown. Wide receivers Anthony Garcia, Johnny Wilson and Benjamin Thompson accounted for 82, 66, and 34 yards receiving, respectively, with Thompson scoring the receiving touchdown.

After the game, Pickering head coach Dan Williams expressed his pleasure with the team and the unexpected win.

"I'm thrilled with how we played tonight," Coach Williams said. "If we play like this all year there's no way we're not going to win the state championship. That was the best I've seen our boys fight. They never gave up, and they were scrambling everywhere for that ball. Five turnovers! That's spectacular!"

CHAPTER 11

THE LOUD-MOUTHED ROOSTER

What do you think?" Sam asked with a smile as he put the phone he'd been reading from back into his pocket. "That'll be the story I put on The Scribbler website tomorrow. Has a nice ring to it, don't you think?"

Caleb chuckled and Jim gave a nervous laugh. The former was holding Chet down on a stool in the science lab while Sam sat on the edge of the teacher's desk at the front and studied him. Jim stood off to the side with a wild look in his eyes, clearly uncomfortable with the situation. Chet glared at Sam, who just smiled back at him before turning to Caleb.

"Everything worked out perfectly," Sam said, beginning to pace back and forth while he addressed the others. "Aaron did exactly what he was supposed to do – throw the game but make it look like he wasn't trying to throw the game. I can give him his cut tomorrow. Looks like you two got a bunch of students to make bets against Pickering, and I got bets from all the teachers around the area Mr. Boreland told me about. I'm surprised how many of them are willing to gamble on high school sports, actually, despite the fact they could get fired for it. I took 12 different bets just on my own, and I know he took some more. He was in charge of the whales. I'm almost positive he got at least one big one for this game – someone from Pickering who was sad about losing those five starters and thought for sure Chetfield would win."

"Really?" Caleb said, wonder on his face. "How much do you think we got? Ten thousand? Fifty thousand?"

Sam looked at Caleb and snorted.

"You dream small, Caleb," the taller boy said. "If Mr. Boreland got as big of whales as I think he did, and with everything you two collected, I'd say we came out with about three-hundred-thousand."

Chet's mouth dropped open, and he saw Caleb smile widely at the news.

"Yes!" Caleb exclaimed, pumping his fist into the air. "That's awesome!"

Sam didn't reply, he just turned his eyes back to Chet.

"It would have been awesome," he said, "if Lord Chetfield hadn't figured it out. What are we going to do about our little intruder?"

"He thinks he's some kind of investigative reporter or something," Caleb sneered. "Looks like he got lucky."

Sam gave Caleb a dirty look.

"He followed you," Sam said in a flat voice. "He didn't get lucky ... you were just stupid."

A myriad of emotions crossed Caleb's face – surprise shame, anger. Hatred burned in his eyes as he took a threatening step toward Chet.

"You followed me?!" Caleb demanded, wrenching Chet's shirt in his fist and twisting him halfway off the stool. "I'm gonna give you another black eye!"

Sam waved a pacifying hand toward Caleb, then gave Chet another considering look.

"You saw Mr. Boreland at the Pickering game last week, didn't you?" he asked. Chet thought about denying it, but decided at this point it didn't make a difference whether or not he told the truth, so he merely nodded. Sam looked at him with a blank expression for a long, drawn-out moment, and Chet began to sweat.

"He was taking bets from their newspaper adviser," Sam finally said. "I've been working on him for the past month, trying to convince him that no one knew about our little sports gambling ring. He's one of the biggest whales we could have gotten. Apparently his father was rich and left him a fortune when he died. And it's a well-known fact that the man likes to gamble. I'm pretty sure he finally came around."

"Did we really make three-hundred-thousand?" Caleb asked quietly. Sam looked at him and nodded.

"We won't get to keep any of it if he rats us out, though," he said, looking meaningfully at the other boys. "In fact, we'd probably have to go to jail."

Jim's eyes widened even more as the implications of Sam's words sank in, and Chet began to realize where things were heading. He felt a slow panic rising up his spine, and he started to breathe rapidly. Just how cruel was Sam? What was he capable of, and what was he going to do to him?

"What are you going to do?" Jim asked, echoing Chet's thoughts. Sam looked at him consideringly.

"You two get out of here," Sam said. "I have to meet up with Mr. B to settle with all the money. Meet me tomorrow morning and we'll wrap everything up."

Caleb looked at Sam with an unreadable expression, then he nodded and gathered Jim, leaving the science lab but closing the door behind them. Now Chet was alone with Sam.

"You've really stepped into it, haven't you?" Sam said, shaking his head. "Just couldn't stop digging. You actually are a pretty decent reporter. But one idiot getting in the way was bad enough. You make two. Nobody will believe two students in two weeks just ran away from home. They might have believed it of Gavin – his home life hasn't been great for a long time – but they'll never believe you just took off, too. So, what am I gonna do with you?"

It took a moment for Sam's words to sink in, and once they did he sat up straight.

"Wait ... what?!" Chet said. "What do you know about Gavin? Do you know where he is?"

Sam just snickered and stared at him consideringly. Then he stood up abruptly and waved his hand toward the door, as if inviting Chet to go with him.

"C'mon, Mr. Investigative Reporter," Sam said. "If you want answers, come with me."

"Where are we going?" Chet asked, hesitant to follow Sam anywhere.

"To the Water Maze," Sam said, continuing to walk toward the door. "Mr. B is waiting for me there."

"The Water Maze?" Chet asked, confused. "Why there?"

Sam stopped in the doorway of the science lab and turned around to face Chet. A slow smile spread across his face.

"Mr. B spends every free moment there," Sam said. "He's searching for the architect's treasure."

Chet blinked once, then again. He felt as if Sam had just punched him in the gut. He blinked a third time and tried to make his brain work properly. Mr. Boreland was searching for the architect's treasure?! And he was searching in the Water Maze? Maybe that's why he was there that night when he caught them snooping around. But what did that have to do with Gavin or sports gambling or Sam?

As a thousand thoughts raced through Chet's mind, Sam just continued to smile at him with a wicked, knowing grin. Then he dropped one more bomb into Chet's already befuddled mind.

"I think he knows what happened to your dad," Sam said quietly ... cruelly. "I'm pretty sure he's planning on skipping out of town tonight, though, so if you want answers you better come with me. It's probably your last chance."

Chet felt himself growing hot with anger and anticipation. Part of him felt like Sam was being purposefully obtuse with his bits of information, but a bigger part of him yearned for information about his father. He'd tried to convince himself to put the past behind him, but just a chance to get some real information suddenly re-ignited that fire within him. With a determined nod, he set his shoulders and then forced himself to take a step toward Sam. The next step was easier, and soon the two of them were walking through the parking lot and getting into Sam's car.

It was silent in the car as Sam drove the short distance to the Water Maze. Unlike earlier, a clarity of thought now permeated Chet's mind. All of the pieces of the puzzle were finally coming together, and a zen-like calmness overcame him. Sam, Caleb and Jim had been collecting bets all year on sports. Sam had bribed Aaron to throw the game. Somehow Mr. Boreland was in on it – or possibly he was the mastermind of the whole gambling ring. They'd made a killing at the homecoming game. But Chet still didn't understand how Gavin fit into everything, or how Mr. Boreland's search for the Architect's treasure fit in. He knew he was close to getting those final pieces of the puzzle, and the buzz of anticipation inside him was a tightly held ball of energy that he hid behind a calm exterior. He was eager to share what he knew with Kaiah. He wondered absently what she was doing at the moment, and whether or not she was worried about him. They were supposed to have met with Jess after the game. He wondered what Jess would do if they didn't show up.

Sam pulled up to the front of the Water Maze and quickly hopped out. Chet followed, and as the two walked through the front doors Chet noticed the red wires snaking around the building. There was a digital display attached to a brown box on the front of the building just above the doors. It read "10:00" in bright red numbers. Chet knew immediately that it was a countdown timer, and he remembered that the building was set to implode that evening. The clock wasn't counting down yet, however, so he assumed they must have some time yet.

Sam started to make his way deeper into the building and Chet stopped, suddenly having second thoughts.

"Wait," Chet said. "He's in there? Why isn't he out here in the front?"

Sam turned toward him and shrugged.

"You'll see," he said. "C'mon."

"But this building is set to explode tonight," Chet said. "What if we get trapped in there?"

Sam snickered and gave him another evil grin.

"I told you it was your last chance," Sam said with a shrug. "Your choice. Stay out here if you want. Or go run back to the school and try to tell somebody, not that anyone will probably believe you. At least, they won't believe you in time to stop the building blowing up. But Mr. B will be long gone before that."

He gave Chet one last meaningful look, then turned and walked down one of the darkened halls. Chet stared after him for a long moment, then quickly hurried to catch up. Sam's cell phone light guided them through the halls. Seeing Sam's cell phone gave him an idea, and he quickly pulled out his own cell phone and started to type a text message to Kaiah.

At the Water Maze with Sam. Mr. Boreland also here. Getting answers ... I hope.

Sam wove his way through the halls and Chet soon got disoriented. There's no way he could have found his way back on his own, and that thought started to make him sweat. A few moments later Chet heard muffled voices in front of them, growing louder as they drew closer. Finally, Sam stopped at a door. He turned to Chet and gave him another cruel grin.

"Here we are," he said. "All your answers are through this door. Are you ready?"

Chet swallowed and then nodded. Sam shook his head ruefully and then opened the door. The voices inside cut off abruptly. When Chet went through the door after Sam, he saw Mr. Boreland standing in the middle of the room, and sitting in a chair off to the side was Gavin. He was tied to the chair, and he looked fairly disheveled if not otherwise in good health.

"Another one?!?" Mr. Boreland exclaimed as soon as he saw Chet. "I told you, Sam, we already have too many clucking chickens who know about this!"

Sam looked taken aback as Mr. Boreland stared daggers at him. Then he adopted an angry scowl of his own.

"What was I supposed to do?" Sam demanded. "Lord Chetfield here figured it all out. He followed Caleb tonight, saw him collecting all the bets, then saw him and Jim gathering all the money together."

"So you brought him here?!?" Mr. Boreland asked.

"I suppose I could have let him go tell Principal Miller everything," Sam said sarcastically.

Mr. Boreland stared at Sam in anger for a long moment, then controlled himself with some effort. Then he turned to face Chet.

"I suppose you want a cut of the money, too?" he asked, frustration and anger flashing through his eyes.

"I don't care about the money," Chet said. "I want to know what you know about my father. And I want to know why you have Gavin tied up here at the Water Maze. Has he been here for the past two weeks?!"

Sam snorted and answered Chet's question.

"Yes," he said flatly. "Pain in the butt to keep bringing him food and water every day. If nothing else I'll be glad for that to be over."

Chet frowned at him, then remembered the conversation he'd overheard between Sam and Mr. Boreland that morning.

"*Feed that loud-mouthed rooster*," Chet said as another piece of the puzzle fell into place. "You were talking about Gavin. You've been keeping him here the whole time. Why?"

Mr. Boreland frowned at him again, then snorted.

"He figured out what we were doing a few weeks ago," he said, shooting Gavin a dirty look. "Sam's dad was dating Gavin's mom, and apparently Gavin overheard Sam talking to his dad about our plans one night. Clever idiot decided to try to blackmail us instead of ratting us out. Like I was gonna let that happen."

"So, what? You kidnapped him and tied him up and brought him to the Water Maze?" Chet asked, genuinely confused. "That doesn't make any sense!"

"He did that later," Gavin said suddenly, anger flashing across his face. "First he stole the map from me."

"Shut up!" Mr. Boreland yelled, taking a threatening step toward Gavin. Chet noticed absently that the older man winced as he took a step, and he favored his leg slightly.

"Why?" Gavin responded defiantly. "You afraid someone else is gonna steal your treasure?"

"Map?" Chet asked. "What map?"

Gavin shot a murderous look at Mr. Boreland, then turned back to Chet.

"The map to that old architect's house," he said. "The one who supposedly has a treasure hidden somewhere."

Chet got very still and had to control his breathing as he considered what Gavin had just said.

"I told you to shut up!" Mr. Boreland said, taking another threatening step toward him. This time he stumbled just the slightest little bit, and again seemed to favor one of his legs. A sudden realization came to Chet like a bolt of lightning.

"It was you!" he exclaimed, pointing a finger at Mr. Boreland. "You're the one who was at the house that night!"

Mr. Boreland blinked once, then gave Chet a frown.

"Yes," he said matter-of-factly.

"What did you find?" Chet demanded. "What do you know about my father?!"

Mr. Boreland looked at him consideringly, then shook his head and shrugged his shoulders.

"I convinced Gavin to meet me after practice one night to work out the particulars of his proposal," Mr. Boreland said. "I had no intentions of letting him blackmail me, but I had to see just how much he knew of what we had planned. I just needed a couple more weeks to get to the homecoming game for our big score, and I was willing to give him a small cut if he kept his mouth shut."

Gavin snorted.

"Yeah, right!" he said. "You were never gonna give me any money. You were just stringing me along."

Mr. Boreland shot Gavin another look, then continued his story.

"I told him I'd let him in if he'd let me know what he knows about the architect's treasure," Mr. Boreland said. "Sam said he had a map to the architect's house, and I wanted to see it."

"Yeah, and then you stole it from me!" Gavin yelled. "All you care about is the big score. Gambling, treasure – it's all money to you."

Sam laughed and Mr. Boreland gave him a glare.

"It's true," Sam said. "You do care an awful lot about money. Don't get me wrong, I like money, too. And Gavin can try to deny it, but he's the biggest gambler of us all."

The three glared at each other without saying anything more, and Chet stood to the side trying to figure out what to say next.

"How'd you get a map of the architect's house?" Chet asked Gavin. It wasn't what he'd intended to ask – he really wanted to know more about his father – but the question had just blurted itself out.

"My dad won it at a poker game," Gavin said without hesitation. "Some dude was bragging about it or something, and my dad convinced him to add it to the pot. He ended up winning. My dad said the other guy was *not* happy."

Chet shook his head and turned back to Mr. Boreland.

"Sam said you know something about my dad," he said. "Do you know how or why he died? Why was he at that house?"

Mr. Boreland frowned and looked at Sam, who just shrugged. Then Mr. Boreland looked back at Chet and shook his head.

"I don't know why he was there," he said. "My guess is he was trying to steal the treasure and he got caught."

"My dad was no thief!" Chet said angrily. Mr. Boreland just chuckled in reply.

"If you say so," he said. "I know he didn't find the treasure, though ... because there was no treasure!"

"What?!" Chet asked, genuinely confused. "But you found something that night at the house. I saw you take something out of the wall."

"Yeah ... this," Mr. Boreland replied, pulling out a piece

of parchment from one of his pockets. "Just another map – a map to this building. But it's half burnt and now you can hardly read it. I've been trying to figure it out for the past two weeks! Stupid thing is driving me nuts!"

Gavin snorted and Mr. Boreland glared at him.

"Wait ... so one map led to another map?" Chet asked.

"Yes," Mr. Boreland replied, clearly frustrated. "And I've been trying to decipher it ever since."

A thought suddenly occurred to Mr. Boreland, and his eyes lit up as he took an excited step toward Chet.

"Your father knew all about this treasure, didn't he?" he said, taking a few more steps toward Chet. "Maybe you can help me figure out this map. We could share the treasure."

"Don't believe him!" Gavin yelled. "He'll just double-cross you, like he double-crossed me!"

"I won't, I promise," Mr. Boreland said, his voice now dripping with false sweetness. "I'm getting out of town tonight. I knew we'd eventually get caught for gambling on sports, and I never had planned on sticking around long enough to get arrested. I'll take our winnings and go, but I'd much rather have the treasure with me, too. Rumors are that the old architect hid millions in old gold coins in one of his buildings. I could hide out in Australia for the rest of my life with that kind of money."

"Now hold on a second," Sam suddenly blurted out. "You're not leaving without giving me and the boys our cut.

We kept your secret this whole time, and we were the ones who took all those bets. I figure we're due at least 25 percent apiece of the winnings. And I think I'll take a cut of that treasure, too, now that you mention it. You'll have to share with Gavin here, too, if you expect him to stay quiet. Especially since you've kept him tied up here for the past two weeks."

"That's an understatement," Gavin said. "I want half, at least!"

"You're in no position to negotiate," Mr. Boreland said. "I could just leave you tied to that chair and cut out of town. I'd be long gone before anyone found you."

"You can't do that!" Chet said. "The building is scheduled to explode tonight! The countdown is supposed to start any minute!"

Mr. Boreland froze and looked at him in shock.

"What?" he asked quietly.

"It's true," Sam said. "Don't you read the newspaper? They've been planning this for the past month. There's a crowd of people already gathered on the baseball field to watch it explode."

Gavin groaned and immediately started straining against his restraints.

"Let me out of here!" he yelled. "You're crazy! You're gonna get me killed!"

Mr. Boreland looked frantic. He looked to Gavin, then to

Sam, then to Chet, then down at the map, and then back up at Chet.

"Help me!" he said. "We can find the treasure together! I know we can. Surely you know something from your dad's investigation!"

"There's no time!" Chet said.

Mr. Boreland looked frantic. Suddenly he shoved the map toward Chet.

"Here," he said. "Just look at it. Tell me if anything on there rings a bell. Surely your dad knew something."

Chet looked at the map in Mr. Boreland's outstretched hand and then slowly reached out his own hand to grab it. Curiosity got the better of him and he began to examine the piece of parchment. What Mr. Boreland had said was true, a good portion of the map had been burned away in the fire at the architect's house and there were holes with missing information. But it was clear that the map was for the Water Maze. Chet remembered wondering what it would look like if someone chopped off the top half of the building and looked down at the maze from above. This map was the answer to that question. It literally looked like one of the old mazes that his mother would give him when he was younger, though this one had scribblings and symbols all over it. In fact, it looked a lot like blueprints that an architect would make.

"What do you want me to do with this?" Chet asked, looking up at Mr. Boreland.

"I traced everything to this room," Mr. Boreland said, "but it's a dead end. There's nothing here – no secret hidey holes or levers that open hidden rooms or anything like that. It's just a room."

Gavin snorted again, this time with a sarcastic chuckle.

"I told you it was a waste of time at the very beginning," Gavin said. "It's just a never-ending game. That old architect was crazy – everybody knew it. And all those people who have been looking for his treasure for years and years are crazy, too. You're just like the rest of them."

"It's not a game!" Mr. Boreland yelled, turning on his heel and glaring at Gavin. "It's real! I know it is! And there are millions hidden in this building."

He turned back to Chet and stared at him pleadingly.

"Please, look again," he begged. "This is our last chance. Think of all the money we could share."

Chet frowned at him. Was this really what his father had died for? Some stupid treasure? Maybe there was more to it than just treasure. Maybe if he could find what the map pointed to he'd get another clue to what his father had been investigating. Slowly, and now with more determination, he looked down at the map.

Chet loved puzzles and maps and riddles. He loved figuring out how to put various pieces together to solve something – it's why he loved investigative reporting. And as he looked down at the map, he gradually began to realize that what the architect had created was essentially a big riddle. Yes, the map did lead to this room, but there were a series of other things within the building that had to be done first before getting to the room.

"Did you push the second stone up from the floor in the front lobby?" Chet asked, looking up at Mr. Boreland.

"What?" the older man asked. "What are you talking about?"

Chet held the map toward him and pointed to a small symbol by the front entrance to the building.

"Right there," Chet said. "You have to do a series of things within the building before you get to this room."

"Huh," Mr. Boreland said. "That makes sense, I guess. I've been in all the other rooms that are marked with those symbols. I even found a couple of levers and hidden push points in the wall, but nothing ever happened."

"That's because you didn't hit the first one in the lobby," Chet said. "How many of these others have you done already?"

Mr. Boreland looked at the map and studied the points within the building that Chet was referring to.

"All of them, actually," Mr. Boreland said, excitement starting to creep into his voice. "All of them except that one in the lobby."

Chet looked at him and raised an eyebrow.

"Well, there's your answer," he said.

"Wait," Gavin said skeptically. "Are you telling me that all he had to do this whole time was push that stone in the lobby and he would have found the treasure?!"

Chet looked at Gavin and then shrugged his shoulders.

"Yep," he said.

Gavin looked at him, dumbfounded, and then Sam started to laugh. Gavin frowned at Sam and then started straining against the ropes again.

"You crazy idiot!" he yelled at Mr. Boreland. "We could have had that treasure weeks ago! Let me out of here!"

Mr. Boreland looked at Gavin consideringly.

"Not yet," he said. "As soon as I find the treasure. I'll give you a cut, just like I promised, as long as you keep your mouth shut long enough for me to get out of town. Same for you, Sam. In fact, why don't you go calm down Caleb and Jim. Make sure they don't say anything to anybody. You know Jim has been getting skittish about all this for the past week."

"I'm not going anywhere," Sam said. "I'm not stupid. You'll find that treasure and bail and not give anything to any of us. I'm staying right here until I get my money."

Mr. Boreland glared at him.

"Fine," he said. "Stay here with Gavin. But give me the cash so that I know you won't just set him free and take off."

Sam gave Mr. Boreland a wry smile that spoke volumes. The two knew each other well enough to know that they'd double-cross the other in a split second. Sam reached into his pocket and pulled out a large wad of cash wrapped in a rubber band. I was the money he, Caleb and Jim had collected from bets – probably close to $50,000, Chet assumed. Mr. Boreland snatched it out of Sam's hand and then quickly stuffed it into his own pocket.

"Me and Chet will be back soon," he said. "Stay here."

Sam nodded, then leaned against the wall and shooed them away with his hand.

"Go on then," he said. "The clock is ticking."

Mr. Boreland looked at Chet, who nodded and then followed the older man out the door and into the maze.

World-renowned architect offers prize of millions to treasure seekers

By Edgar Scheffield
New York Times · Correspondent

NEW YORK, NY – One of the world's most preimenent architect's has set the world on fire with a promise of millions in gold coins that he has hidden in one of his buildings somewhere around the world.

Swedish architect Alsbet Samuelsson has designed more than 100 buildings in most of the major cities around the world. His style is progressive with a flare for the dramatic, and he has gained a reputation for being one of the most sought-after architects around the globe. Earlier this month Samuelsson announced that he had been strategically and systematically placing clues into each of his building designs that would lead treasure-seekers to the ultimate prize: a bronze chest filled with rare gold coins that he says are worth in excess of $1 million.

Samuelsson's announcement comes in the wake of a revelation from the son of New York governor, Charles Evans Hughes, who claims to have been the first to discover one of the architect's hidden clues in his family's mansion.

"Mr. Samuelsson was hired five years ago by our family to design an ultra-modern mansion," Charles Evans Hughes Jr. said. "After we moved in two years ago, I became aware of some intricate designs in many of the capitals at the tops of the columns. These designs looked like symbols of some sort, and when I mentioned them to a friend of mine one day he suggested that they were architect's marks. I became increasingly curious, especially after I noticed them in other parts of the house. Imagine my surprise when one day I pushed on one of the symbols and a secret compartment was opened in the wall! Inside I found a map to another buliding. I, of course, immediately contacted Mr. Samuelsson, and he confirmed that there was, indeed, a treasure hidden somewhere in one of his buildings, and that I had found one of his clues!"

The notion of Samuelsson hiding a treasure in one of his buildings – with clues and riddles to help guide the way – has come as no surprise to those who know him best. Many have noted how eccentric he is, and have even gone so far as to call him "crazy" at certain points.

"The man is a loon," said Jack Brand, head of the U.S. Architect's Society, with headquarters in New York. "Many of his designs are impossible to build. They defy the laws of physics, yet he forces contractors to try them anyway. It costs families and companies a lot of money to attempt to create his designs, and at the end of the day they almost always fail. It wouldn't surprise me if there's actually no treasure at all and he's just created an elaborate game for his own amusement!"

Samuelsson declined to comment for this report, but he did confirm unequivocally that the treasure does exist and that it is indeed hidden in one of his buildings

CHAPTER 12

THE SAMUELSEEKERS

Mr. Boreland took back the newspaper clipping from Chet and carefully re-folded it, gently putting it back in his wallet. It was an old newspaper report from 1909, and Chet had handled it gently so as not to damage it any further than it had already been damaged. The faded yellow newsprint was barely holding itself together, but it was still intact enough for someone to read the article.

"So you believe it?" Chet asked skeptically as they made their way through the dark halls of the Water Maze. Chet had used his phone flashlight to read the article. He had noticed that there were multiple messages from Kaiah on his phone, but he hadn't taken the time yet to respond to her. He wasn't sure what he wanted to tell her, and he didn't want her rushing into the Water Maze after him.

"Well, obviously," Mr. Boreland replied. "Why else would I be here? That was a dumb question."

Chet frowned.

"And you're telling me my dad was one of these treasure seekers?" Chet pressed. "What did you call them?"

"The Samuelseekers," Mr. Boreland replied. "They're all over the world. I'm not sure how many of them there are, but I'd guess thousands. Any time you're around one of Alsbet Samuelsson's buildings you'll likely run into one of them. They're constantly trying to find clues to the treasure. Sometimes they'll even break into private buildings just to look for clues. I assume that's what your father was doing when he died."

"I don't think so," Chet said. "I'm pretty sure he didn't actually care about the treasure. I think he was investigating something else."

"What makes you say that?" Mr. Boreland asked.

"Most of the notes I've read in his office had more to do with different businesses and stuff," Chet said. "I think he only investigated the Samuelseekers because they started to overlap with other things he was researching."

"But why would he break into the architect's house if not to search for the treasure?" Mr. Boreland asked.

"I don't know," Chet answered. "There could be a million reasons why. What I want to know is why the architect lived in Chetfield, Ohio!"

"He didn't," Mr. Boreland said. "At least, the original Als-bet Samuelsson didn't. His grandson, Axel Samuelsson, is the one who built the mansion here. He fell in love with a woman from this area, and as they grew older her parents' health was fading. He built her the house here so that they could be closer to her parents. But once her parents died, they started traveling around the world. That's why no one was there when your father broke into – er, was at the house when it burned."

"If no one was there, what started the fire?" Chet said. "And why would my father get caught in there? Someone else *had* to be there! Someone killed him and started the fire!"

Chet stopped in the middle of the hall and turned to glare at Mr. Boreland. The older man took a startled step back and then glared right back at him.

"Sure, if you say so, kid," Mr. Boreland said. "Can we keep moving, please? I don't want to get buried in this building when it blows."

Chet scowled at him, then turned around and started leading them down the hall again. The maze twisted and turned and Chet was reminded of the chase through these halls a week earlier.

"You're probably right about somebody else being there," Mr. Boreland said suddenly, startling Chet. "It's not the first time someone has died searching for Samuelsson's treasure. In fact, quite a few people have died over the years."

"Really?" Chet asked, looking over his shoulder at the older man.

"Yes," Mr. Boreland said.

Chet considered this information and wondered what his father could have gotten mixed up in on that fateful evening. Something defiant inside him refused to believe that his father was one of the Samuelseekers and that he'd broken into the mansion that night just to steal some treasure. His father wouldn't have done that. He was certain that his dad had been following a lead for his investigation, and something had happened.

"That's really all you know?" Chet asked Mr. Boreland. "Sam said you knew about my father and how he died."

"I think Sam over-sold it," Mr. Boreland said with a sarcastic chuckle. "I've told you everything I know, kid."

"Which is a fat lot of nothing," Chet replied angrily. "I don't care about this stupid treasure! The only reason I came here with Sam was to learn something about my dad, and now it turns out that was a waste of time. Why don't you just let Gavin go and we can all get out of here?!"

"Not yet," Mr. Boreland said. "Treasure first."

Chet growled in reply but kept working his way through the halls. Every once in a while they would come to one of the four-way junctures and Chet would have to pull out the map to try to figure out which way to go. Every time they did that it made him increasingly nervous, as the boxes of explosives placed at the tops of the walls were now blinking with red lights. He'd been careful not to trip on any of the wires snaking across the floor as they walked, but the blinking lights made him afraid that the countdown had already started.

After determining which way to go at yet another four-way intersection, Chet continued on. They'd been walking the halls for a good five minutes. Chet looked at the time on his cell phone and saw that it was now a good half hour past the end of the football game. He wasn't sure how long it would take for everyone to get into place on the baseball field to watch the explosion, but he assumed the demolition company wouldn't wait much longer to start the process. He tried to quicken his step while still being careful where he placed his feet between the wires.

A minute later they made their way out of the maze and into the front lobby. It was more well-lit in the front thanks to the windows, which let in light from the moon.

"Good job," Mr. Boreland said. "Now which stone are we supposed to push?"

Chet looked at the map. It really did look very much like an architect's blueprints, and if he was reading it correctly then the stone they had to push was almost all the way on the extreme edge of the wall. Chet started walking toward it, but then heard something outside that made him jump. A car door slammed. Both Chet and Mr. Boreland froze and looked out the window to see four people climbing out of a beat-up brown car. Chet was surprised to see Chunk, Kaiah and Noélle get out of the car with Jess, who had been driving. The four of them made their way to the front door and hurried inside.

"Chet!" Kaiah exclaimed, rushing toward him. The others followed behind her quickly.

"What are you guys doing here?!" Chet asked.

"We're here to help you rescue Gavin!" Kaiah said.

"Yeah, where is he?" Jess said, pushing her way forward. "Jim said this is where Mr. Boreland has been keeping him. What did you do to him?!"

She shoved a finger into Mr. Boreland's chest. He took a step back as he glared at her and the others.

"Jim ..." Mr. Boreland said. "I knew he'd spill the beans."

"Oh, he spilled the beans, alright," Chunk said. "Said you've been gambling on games! Said you blackmailed Aaron to throw the game tonight! How could you?!"

Mr. Boreland just sneered back at Chunk before turning to Chet.

"Let's finish this," he said. "Move it."

"Finish what?" Jess said. "What's going on here? I want to know where Gavin is!"

"He's in the maze," Chet said, trying to mollify the older girl. "Give me a minute and I'll take you to him."

Jess frowned at him and started to say something else, then nodded.

"You better hurry up," Noélle said into the silence. "The countdown has already started."

"What?!" Chet exclaimed. "How much time is left?!"

Chunk jumped and ran back to the front doors, leaning outside and looking up at the digital clock above him.

"That's not good," the bigger boy said, pointing up to the wires above the door. Chet looked up, as well, and saw that there was a brown rectangular package taped above the door. "It's already less than eight minutes!"

Chet turned to Mr. Boreland.

"There's no time!" he yelled. "Forget the treasure! We've got to get Gavin and get out of here."

"No!" Mr. Boreland yelled back. "We can still do this. Go push the stone! Quick!"

Chet growled in frustration and then turned back to the wall. He worked his way along the wall and looked at the map, trying to figure out which stone to push.

"What are you doing?" Kaiah asked.

"Looking for a specific stone," Chet said. "If you push it then it should release some kind of lever back in the room where Gavin is, and that should open a secret compartment where the treasure is hidden.

"Treasure?" Chunk asked, a note of excitement in his

voice. "What treasure? Are we talking like gold and jewels and stuff."

Chet looked over his shoulder at his friend and nodded.

"Yes," Chet said. "I'll explain later."

"If we're gonna do this, we better hurry!" Kaiah said.

Chet nodded, and continued to search for the right stone. He ran his hands along the wall and counted the stones according to what the map suggested. Eventually he found the stone that he thought had to be the right one, and gave it a good push. Amazingly, the stone moved. Chet leaned into it more and the stone pushed even farther into the wall. The more he pushed, the deeper the recess became until finally the stone fell away and Chet could reach through the wall. He felt some kind of a handle inside.

"I think I found the lever," Chet said.

"Well, pull it!" Mr. Boreland said excitedly.

Chet grabbed the handle and tried to pull, but nothing happened. He tried to twist it to the left, and again nothing happened. When he tried to twist it to the right, however, it started to budge. He twisted harder and suddenly the lever gave way with a loud *click*! At the same time, something clamped down on his wrist from above and held his hand in place. It didn't hurt, but he couldn't pull his hand out of the hole. He tried to yank his arm out, but it wouldn't budge.

"I'm stuck!" he exclaimed in fear. "I can't get my arm out!"

A moment later a loud grinding noise started to come through the wall. Mr. Boreland jumped back and looked toward the entrance hall into the water maze from which he and Chet had just exited moments earlier.

"There's a door sliding across the entrance!" Mr. Boreland said. "It's blocking the way back!"

He raced toward the hallway as the grinding continued. From the sound of it the sliding door was picking up momentum, moving faster. Just as Mr. Boreland was about to jump into the hall, the door slammed shut and blocked his way.

The sudden silence was unnerving, and all of Chet's friends looked at each other in fear. Mr. Boreland took a few steps back and then looked at the group of students with defeat on his face. He began to back his way toward the front doors.

"Hey!" Chet yelled. "Where are you going? Gavin's still in there! We have to find a way to get him out!"

Chet tried to pull his hand out again, and again he had no luck. Mr. Boreland quickened his pace and before anyone could do anything to stop him, he ran out the door. They watched in shock as he jumped into his car and drove away.

"Coward," Chunk said.

"Chunk, go see how much time we have left," Chet said, trying yet again to pull his arm free. "Noélle, Jess, go get some help from somebody."

"No way!" Jess said. "I'm not leaving here without Gavin!"

"You're the only one who can drive!" Chet said.

Jess just shook her head stubbornly and crossed her arms.

"It's OK," Noélle said. "I can drive. Jess, give me your keys."

Jess frowned at her, then reluctantly handed over the keys.

"The clock says less than seven minutes!" Chunk yelled frantically from the front door.

"Hurry, Noélle," Chet said. "Go get help."

Her eyes got big, but she adopted a look of determination before turning and running on her little legs. She burst through the door, hopped into Jess' car and then took off down the drive. By the time she was gone, Chunk had made his way back to Chet's side and was trying to help him get his arm out.

"Kaiah, look at the map," Chet said, nodding to the map that had fallen to the ground in front of him. "Surely there's another way into the maze. The architect wouldn't have just closed off the maze without providing another way to the treasure."

Kaiah jumped forward and picked up the map. She frowned as she studied it, clearly confused by what she was seeing.

"What are all these markings here?" she asked, pointing to some symbols in the bottom corner of the map.

"I think they're architect's symbols," Chet said, "but I don't know what they mean."

Chunk was trying frantically to get his fingers through the hole around Chet's arm to pull it free, but there was just not enough space to wiggle through. Chet kept trying to pull his hand free, but there was no give.

"This part looks like a mathematical equation," Kaiah said. "Give me a minute, I think I can figure it out."

"We don't really have a minute," Chet said.

Kaiah didn't respond. Instead, she closed her eyes and started mumbling to herself. Chet could barely hear her, but it sounded like she was rambling off random numbers. After a few seconds her eyes popped open.

"Got it!" she yelled. "3-6-4-2!"

"Ok ..." Chet said. "What does that mean."

Kaiah looked at him and the excitement faded from her eyes.

"I don't know," she said.

"Maybe it's a combination," Jess said suddenly. "Does anybody see a lock anywhere?"

Chunk popped up and started looking along the wall for some kind of lock or number dial. Kaiah did the same, and Jess ran to the other end of the room to look there. Chet kept trying to free his arm. He didn't want to add anymore to the fear his friends were already feeling, but a rising panic was starting to crawl up his stomach and throughout the rest of his body. He was barely holding back a desperate wail that wanted to escape through his lips. He did not want to die – especially not by being buried underneath a building. That seemed like one of the worst ways to die he could ever imagine.

Kaiah suddenly raced back to him.

"Why would your hand be trapped *AND* there be a door blocking our way?" she asked. "That doesn't make sense!"

Chet frowned up at her and considered what she was saying.

"You're right," he said. "That doesn't make sense. Why would the architect want someone's hand trapped at all?"

"I think it's a riddle," Kaiah said. "Can you still feel the handle?"

Chet reached his fingers forward and immediately felt the handle he'd turned earlier. He took it in his grip and looked up at her and nodded.

"Ok ... try this," she said. "Try turning the handle like it's the hand of a clock. Start with 3 o'clock, then 6, then 4, then 2."

A spark of hope blossomed inside Chet as he nodded at her. He turned the handle to his best approximation of 3 o'clock, then followed with the others – 6, 4 and 2. Nothing happened at first, but then the clamp on the top of his arm pulled away and he was able to pull his arm out. At the same time, a section of wall to their left slid open and revealed a new hallway into the maze.

"That hall's not on the map!" Kaiah said.

"I don't care!" Chet said, leaping up and heading toward the new hall. "It leads back toward Gavin. Let's go!"

Chunk and Jess raced back toward them, but Chunk stopped suddenly by the front doors and peeked yet again at the digital clock.

"How much time?" Chet asked, pulling out his cell phone and opening the timer app.

"5:59 ... 5:58 ... 5:57," Chunk read off, looking at them with fear spread across his face. Chet set his timer to coincide with the explosion countdown.

"Let's go!" Jess yelled, not stopping to look back as she raced down the new hallway. Kaiah looked at Chet, who shrugged and encouraged her to follow Jess. A moment later Chunk caught up to them and they all made their way into the Water Maze.

WARNING!
NOTICE OF DEMOLITION!

This letter is to serve as the required 21-day notification that our company will be doing explosive demolition at this site. As per Chetfield Code of Ordinances, Section 17-195 Construction Site Management, we are required to notify all people to remain at least 1,000 yards away from this property.

Demolition will start no sooner than 21 days from the date of this letter, and take approximately 48 hours following the explosive collapse of the building. If you would like to have a pre-demolition inspection by a licensed engineer or city-approved inspector prior to us commencing with the demolition, please notify our office immediately. If you would like to have on-site seismic monitoring during the demolition, please notify our office immediately.

Please note, any injury resulting in the unlawful entry of this property during the demolition period will be at the violator's own risk. Our company will not be liable for any injuries associated with the unlawful trespass of this building or the surrounding area, which includes the entirety of the demolition site.

To contact our offices, please call 555-291-7878.

CHAPTER 13

FOOTPRINTS IN THE DUST

Chet crumpled up the warning notice and tossed the wadded-up ball of paper into the hall behind them. The paper was the same one Aaron had torn off the door a week earlier. As they'd run into the strange new hallway it had stuck to the bottom of his shoe. It was a ridiculous thing to think about considering their present circumstances.

It was a narrow hall, barely wide enough for one person to fit in, and as such they were forced to go down it one by one. But unlike the rest of the Water Maze, this hallways seemed to have only one path – there were no twists or turns or four-way intersections with multiple options that could lead them into dead ends.

"What are we doing?" Chunk asked, wheezing as he ran.

"We have to find Gavin and get out of here," Chet said. "But I don't know where he is… somewhere in this building."

"In this maze?!" Chunk blurted. "There's no way we'll find him before that timer gets to zero! How much time do we have left?"

Chet shook his head and pulled his phone out of his pocket. It ticked below four minutes. Ahead of them, Jess' cell phone flashlight guided the way through the long, straight hallway.

"You don't want to know," Chet said to his friend.

It was dark, but unlike any of the other halls there were no wires or explosives lining the walls. He glanced at his phone timer again.

3:49 … 3:48 … 3:47.

Chet could hear Kaiah and Chunk shuffling along behind him, the bigger boy still huffing loudly as he tried to catch his breath. Chet realized that Chunk had just finished playing an entire football game – an intense one, at that – and was probably exhausted.

"Why did you guys come here, by the way?" Chet asked.

Chunk just grunted again, letting Kaiah be the one to answer.

"When you didn't come find me after the halftime show I figured you'd done something stupid, like follow Sam or something," she said.

He looked over his shoulder at her with a sheepish grin. She was giving him a look that spoke volumes about what she thought of him not taking her advice to avoid Sam and Mr. Boreland.

"I followed Caleb, actually," he said lamely, shrugging uncomfortably. "Same difference, I suppose."

Chunk snorted, and Kaiah gave Chet a flat stare.

"Well, I looked for you in the stands and couldn't find you," she said. "I found Noélle and your mom, and they said you'd left to wish me luck for the halftime show. … That was very nice, by the way. Thank you."

Chet blushed, embarrassed by the sudden awkwardness. The hall forced them to turn left and Chet didn't hesitate. He looked at his timer and saw that it was now below three-and-a-half minutes. He quickened his step.

"Anyway, after the game I decided to hang by the locker rooms cuz I thought you'd probably go there to meet Chunk," she continued. "Chunk saw me and told me to wait for him while he got out of his uniform. When he came back out we went looking for you. We saw your mom again. She said she was gonna wait for you by the car."

"My mom is probably freaking out right now," Chet said absently. They reached another turn. Chet stood still for a moment and strained his ears, trying to hear for Sam or Gavin's voices. It was eerily silent, however, and after a deep breath Jess turned to the left.

"I told Chunk we should check if you'd maybe gone to meet Jess out front, like we'd planned," Kaiah said. "When we found her, though, you weren't there. So I thought maybe we should look in the science labs. I figured Mr. Boreland was involved considering all we'd figured out, and that was the best I could think of. But you weren't there, either. It was Chunk's idea to look in the newspaper office, which is where we ran into Jim. And, of course, he told us everything."

"Just like that?" Chet asked. "He just blurted everything out and ratted everybody out. Where was Caleb?"

"I might have given him some encouragement," Chunk said, cracking his knuckles in his other hand for emphasis. "I don't know where Caleb was. Haven't seen him or Sam."

Chet looked back at them and nodded in thanks.

"Sam said he was gonna bring me here with Mr. Boreland," Chet explained. "He told me Mr. Boreland had all the answers – including answers about my dad. Mr. Boreland was the one who was at the architect's house that night, by the way. And he really did find something."

"Really?!" Chunk asked. "So your dad was right about the treasure?"

"I still don't think that's what my dad was investigating," Chet said. "And anyway it doesn't explain why he died or what started the fire."

"But there's really a treasure?" Chunk said, excitement in his voice.

"Maybe," Chet said. "We don't know yet. Mr. Boreland found a map at the architect's house – a map to this building. He's been searching this building every day for the past two weeks trying to find this supposed treasure, with no luck."

"Wow!" Chunk said. "And you just walked in tonight and solved it in less than an hour! Ha!"

Chet didn't know what to say, so he just shrugged.

"How much did they make on the bets tonight?" Kaiah asked.

"Three hundred thousand," Chet said matter-of-factly.

"Three hundred thousand?!" Chunk yelled, incredulous.

"Yeah," Chet said. "Crazy, right? Sam, Caleb and Jim all think they're gonna get a cut of the money, but they're all planning on double-crossing each other. Gavin tried to blackmail them, I guess, but that kind of back-fired on him, obviously."

Jess stopped long enough to turn around and glare at Chet. Then she shook her head in frustration and turned back around and continued down the hall.

"So why did he come here?" Kaiah asked. "Why wouldn't he just leave town immediately? He could have just taken the three-hundred-thousand and got out of town!"

"He wanted the treasure," Chet said. "It's stuck in his head, like a fever. It's all he can think about. I'm surprised he ran off, actually. I thought for sure he'd wait to the very last minute trying to get that treasure."

They raced around the next corner and didn't even hesitate at the next turn as they ran left into the darkness. Jess paused for a moment to get her bearings, and in the silence as they stood there panting they all heard a muffled yell from in front of them. They shared a surprised look, then Chet brightened as he realized what the sound was.

"It's Gavin!" he said. "It has to be!"

They rushed forward and came to a dead-end. The hallway had continued to narrow as they'd gone deeper into the building, and at this juncture Chunk had to stand sideways to fit. There was a wild look in his eyes, and Chet couldn't blame him considering he felt claustrophobic himself. Jess groaned as she slapped her hand against the wall.

"Let me look," Chet said, and Jess moved awkwardly out of the way so that he could get a closer look. Chet ran his hands along the wall, feeling along all the creases and looking for some kind of symbol. Suddenly his fingers brushed against something carved into the wall, and when he shone his light on it he saw that it was a symbol like what was on the architect's map. Without hesitation he pushed on the symbol and immediately the wall swung open like a door.

Sam and Gavin turned to them in shock as they all burst into the room. Gavin was still tied in the chair, but Sam was by the main door of the room, his hand on the doorknob.

"Jess?!" Gavin said, confusion on his face. "What are you doing here? And where's Mr. Boreland?

"He took off when the timer started," Jess replied, rushing forward to start picking at Gavin's bonds. "And what do you think I'm doing here? I'm rescuing you."

"Ha," Gavin said. "Thanks. Wait ... the timer started?!"

Chet looked at his phone timer. It now said they had less than a minute-and-a-half. Suddenly the door to the secret entrance started to close. Sam made a panicked sound from deep in his chest.

"Hold that door!" he yelled, pointing behind them.

Chet looked over his shoulder just as the secret entrance slid closed again.

"It doesn't matter," Chet said, rushing forward to help Jess with Gavin's ropes. "We'll get out the other way."

"We can't!" Sam screamed. "This door is locked closed!"

"What?!" Chet yelled.

"A few minutes ago we heard a loud *click* and that little section of the wall over there opened up," Sam said, pointing to the other side of the room where a rectangular hole about a foot wide and a foot tall opened into the side of the wall. "At the same time that opened, this door locked closed. I've been trying to get it open, but it won't budge!"

"Move!" Chunk demanded, pushing Sam out of the way. He then took a running leap and slammed into the door with his shoulder. Chet tried to focus on Gavin's bonds as Chunk rubbed his shoulder and then took a few steps back and launched himself at the door again.

"What was in the hole?" Chet asked as he continued pulling at Gavin's ropes. Mr. Boreland had tied Gavin in such a way that he couldn't escape on his own, and it wasn't easy to untie the knots he'd created. Chet wished he had a knife, and he smiled when he heard Jess mumble something about a knife, as well.

"I don't know," Sam said. "I haven't looked yet."

Kaiah made her way over to the hole in the wall and looked inside.

"Careful!" Chet yelled. "Watch out for more booby traps! Don't get your hand stuck!"

Kaiah flinched back, but then leaned down and peered inside.

"I don't see any treasure box or anything, but there is a piece of paper or something in there," she said. "I'm gonna try to grab it."

"No! Don't!" Chet exclaimed, but she ignored him and did it anyway, reaching her hand in quickly like a snake striking at someone's ankles, then pulling it back quickly with the paper in her hand. A small door snapped closed on the hidey hole with a sharp *snick*.

Chet was finally was able to get a strand of Gavin's rope loose, which was enough to loosen the rest of the knot, and shortly afterward he had Gavin's hands free. The older boy looked Chet in the eyes.

"Thanks," he said, reaching out a hand to Chet. "I'm Gavin."

"I know," Chet said, shaking Gavin's hand briefly. "I'm Chet. This is Kaiah and Chunk. Sorry it took us so long to figure out where you were."

"Chet and Chunk?" he asked, incredulous. "Really?"

Chet just nodded and Chunk spared a glance to grin at him.

"Who are you guys?" Gavin asked, looking at Kaiah as Jess continued to struggle with the knots by his feet.

"We're the News Hawks," Kaiah said proudly, smiling at Chet as she said it. Gavin blinked and seemed confused.

"Can we maybe talk about this later?!" Chunk said, turning away from the door and taking a few steps toward them. "We have to get out of here!"

Chet looked at him frantically, watching as his friend slammed his meaty shoulder repeatedly into the door. He glanced down at Jess and saw that she'd finally managed to get Gavin's feet untied. The senior boy stood up from the chair and rubbed his wrists, wincing in pain. Jess stood up, too, looking worriedly at Chet.

"How much time do we have?" she asked with a tremor in her voice. Chet looked down at the timer on his phone.

"Less than a minute," Chet said weakly.

Chunk heard him and stopped pounding on the door

long enough to share a terror-filled look with his friend. Then, the terror melted from his face and he adopted a look of determination like Chet had never seen on his friend's face before. He turned to the door, took three steps back and then rushed forward, turning at the last minute to slam the door with his shoulder. He bounced off, but not before the door made a crunching sound. Chet noticed that the hinges moved slightly.

"That worked!" Chet exclaimed. "Do it again!"

Chunk scurried back three steps and then slammed into the door a second time. It made another crunching sound, and the others noticed how the hinges moved slightly. Both Kaiah and Jess began to join Chet in offering encouragement to Chunk, who backed up a third time and charged toward the door. He looked like a bull slamming stubbornly into a brick wall, but every time he did so that wall seemed to move a quarter of an inch. Chet knew that if his friend could hit it enough times the hinges would tear away.

Chunk continued to slam into the door – *Bam! Bam! Bam!* It creaked and crunched and the hinges started making grinding sounds as they strained against their brackets. There was a strange sound from just outside the door – as if something big had fallen onto the ground – and they all shared a hopeful smile. Then Chunk took one last lunge at the door and slammed as hard as he could. It broke free with a loud crash, and Chunk fell through the door frame on top of the door, which was now in two pieces.

There was a long moment of silence as they all stared at Chunk, and into that silence came the worst sound they could have possibly heard in that moment …

… Chet's timer rang.

"MOVE!" Chet screamed, and Kaiah, Jess, Sam and Gavin jumped into action. They all rushed out of the room and raced down the hall with the light from Chet's phone leading the way.

They reached the end of the hallway and had the option to go left or right.

"Which way?!" Chet said frantically.

"Left!" Kaiah said, and Chet started to turn that way.

"Wait!" Chunk yelled, pulling them up short. "Look!"

Chet turned back to his friend and pointed his light in Chunk's direction. The bigger boy was pointing to the ground, and when Chet shone the light down he saw footprints in the dust. There were a lot of them, and it took a moment for Chet to realize it was the footprints they'd made when they'd snuck through the building a week earlier.

"We can follow them back to the window!" Chunk said.

Chet didn't even hesitate. He rushed forward, shining the light on the ground to illuminate the footprints. As he followed them around one corner after another, he glanced up at the flashing boxes lining the ceiling. He knew that they could blow at any moment.

It seemed like minutes passed before they reached the room with the broken window, but it had to have only been seconds. Chet didn't have to say anything when they got there – everyone knew instinctively to jump through the window. As Gavin started to climb over the windowsill, Chet saw Chunk grab Kaiah from behind and literally throw her through the window. Jess dove through the window head-first like she was diving into a swimming pool, and Sam hopped over sideways like someone from an old Western movie. Chet put his hands on the ledge and swung his legs over in a kind of side-vault, and landed awkwardly on the ground, scraping his knee as he slammed into the dirt.

A loud *thump* sounded from somewhere deep inside the building behind them, and the ground suddenly shook. The sound of glass shattering soon followed, and then there were many *thumps.* Chet rolled over and looked back at the building. Chunk flipped over the side of the window sill as a thick cloud of dust and debris burst out behind him. A second later Chet couldn't see anything as a huge dirt cloud covered everything around them.

Chet coughed and covered his mouth with his shirt, squinting and blinking the tears out of his eyes as he sat up. He wondered absently why there wasn't any fire or massive explosion, but he assumed construction demolition didn't work that way. He shook his head and scrambled across the ground in the direction he'd seen Kaiah. A minute later they conked heads – she had been crawling toward him, as well.

"Chunk!" Chet yelled, reaching out to grab Kaiah's hand and help her stand up. "Chunk, where are you?!"

"Here," his friend called out immediately, his voice dripping in pain. "I think something's broken."

"What's broken?!" Chet asked frantically, walking toward the sound of his friend's voice.

"Everything …" Chunk groaned. Something in his voice let Chet know Chunk was exaggerating, and he laughed. A moment later he found his friend lying on the ground. Kaiah was still holding his hand. He didn't want to let go.

"I don't know how many explosions there are supposed to be," Chet said. "Do you think maybe you could get up so we can get out of here?"

Chunk groaned again but sat up, and Kaiah and Chet awkwardly helped the bigger boy stand up.

"Where's Gavin and Jess?" Chunk asked as they started to walk away from the building … or what was left of it. There were still more *thumps* exploding at various places around the building, and Chet didn't think it was a good idea to stay too close to the old water plant.

"We're here," Gavin said from off to their left. "Keep walking toward my voice and you'll be out of the dirt cloud in a minute."

The three of them complied, and true to his word they eventually came to an area where the cloud of dirt had mostly dissipated. Gavin was standing there waiting for him, his arm around Jess, who had a gash across her forehead that was bleeding and another on her elbow that was dripping blood onto the ground. But she was smiling, and it seemed as if she couldn't take her eyes off Gavin. That look convinced Chet of something he'd suspected about Jess from the beginning – that she and Gavin were more than merely best friends. It made him think of his own friendship with Kaiah. Chet looked at her and saw that she had scrapes across her cheek and all along the arm of the hand he was holding.

"You OK?" he asked, and she nodded quietly. He started to let go of her hand, but she squeezed tighter, holding onto him as if he was an anchor for her in that moment.

"Where's Sam?" Gavin asked, and everyone started looking around for the other boy. They searched for a few minutes as more explosions sounded from inside the building. The cloud of dirt and debris became so thick, however, that they were forced to move farther and farther away from the building.

"Can we get out of here please?" Chunk asked. Chet nodded, then turned toward the front of the building and started walking. They'd only taken a few steps when they heard the sound of sirens coming down the dirt drive toward the building. There were still more *thumps* coming from the building, but they were tapering off. Just as they reached the front of the building and turned the corner, the explosion sounds stopped, and everything became quiet. A moment later three police cars pulled up. Officers rushed out of the cars and ran toward them. An ambulance came down the drive a few seconds later, followed by Chet's mom's car and then a steady stream of other cars.

"Where's Sam?" Kaiah asked, echoing Gavin's question from earlier as she looked around for some sign of their editor. Chet blinked and then frowned as he looked around as well.

"I don't see his car," Chet said. "He must have taken off."

"Yeah, well, he's not gonna get away," Gavin said fiercely, turning toward one of the officers running toward them. "Neither is Mr. Boreland. Hey, you … officer! I've got something you're gonna want to hear!"

Chet watched as Gavin and Jess started talking with the officers, Gavin gesticulating dramatically while Jess held tightly to his arm as if she was never going to let him go. Chet then turned and looked back at the water maze. The building was rubble, and he couldn't help but feel a stab of disappointment that yet another building associated with his father's investigation was now destroyed.

"What was in that hole?" Chet asked Kaiah quietly.

Kaiah pulled the piece of paper she'd grabbed out of her back pocket and showed it to Chet. It was a thicker piece of parchment that was folded up, and as Chet unfolded it he saw that it was yet another map to another building.

"Another map?" Chet quipped disbelievingly. "Really? That architect really was nutso."

"Are you OK?" Kaiah asked. She was still holding his hand, and he didn't want her to let go.

"Yes," he answered hesitantly. "I was just hoping to get more answers about my dad, is all."

"So, Mr. Boreland didn't tell you anything?" Chunk asked.

Chet squinted as he considered Chunk's words. It was strange that Gavin's dad had won a map to the architect's house at a poker game. Who was the person who had the map in the first place, and why was he betting it as collateral at a poker game? And what did that person know about his father's investigation and death?

"No," Chet answered simply. "Nothing."

They stood there quietly for a long moment. Kaiah's hand felt good in his and helped him push past the lump in his throat. She looked up at him and gave him her best smile, squeezing his hand and leaning her head against his shoulder. Chunk grunted a half-laugh at them, and Chet's face flushed as he looked at his friend. Chet reached up and smacked his friend on the shoulder – the same shoulder he'd used to slam into the door. Chunk winced.

"Ouch!" Chunk said. "That hurts when you do that!"

The two friends laughed.

Missing CHS Student Found!

Science teacher Michael Boreland arrested on charges of kidnapping, attempted murder and child endangerment

By Chet Sayer, Kaiah Dufresne, Noélle Lumiér and Justin "Chunk" Edwards
The Scribbler · Reporters

CHETFIELD, OH – A science teacher at Chetfield High School was arrested Saturday on charges of kidnapping, child endangerment, attempted murder, and gambling. His was the first of five other arrests that took place over the weekend after a state investigation uncovered an illegal sports betting operation that involved teachers, students and administrators from multiple schools. More arrests are likely as the investigation continues and new information comes to light implicating an ever-widening circle of teachers and students, with estimates as high as 50 people involved in the gambling ring.

Michael Boreland has been identified as the chief mastermind behind the gambling ring, as well as the person responsible for the disappearance of CHS senior Gavin Brigantz, whose mother reported him missing more than two weeks ago. Brigantz was found alive in the old water plant mere moments before it was set to explode in a pre-arranged demolition of the decrepit building. Boreland is accused of kidnapping Brigantz and keeping him bound in the water plant. According to sources, Boreland intended to flee the state after collecting winnings in excess of $300,000 he gained from the CHS Homecoming game – a game he actively worked to rig in his favor. Sources indicate Boreland hoped the explosion of the building would kill Gavin and eliminate the primary witness against him.

Boreland has been a teacher at CHS for five years, working primarily in the science department but also serving as an assistant coach for the school's baseball team. He was taken into custody early Saturday afternoon after state troopers found him on I-70 attempting to flee the state.

Sam Chapin, 18 – a CHS student and editor of the school's newspaper The Scribbler – was also arrested on gambling charges. According to officials, Chapin admitted to being Boreland's primary accomplice. Chapin took a plea deal from the District Attorney that offered him a reduced sentence in exchange for information about the gambling ring. Chapin's information led to the arrest of James Doerring, 42, another CHS teacher, and Elvin Dockery, a teacher at Pickering High School and the adviser for the PHS newspaper. Two other students from CHS have also been arrested. Both of them are minors, and as such the police have not released their identities. Detectives have refused to release any other names that might have been implicated by Chapin's information, citing the sensitive nature of the ongoing investigation.

The five were arrested by the Ohio State Police's Statewide Organized Crime Investigative Task Force, which has been conducting an ongoing investigation into suspicious activities around high school athletics for the past two years. According to State Commissioner Bill Roderick, the case was broken open with the help of some student journalists at CHS, who had been conducting an investigation of their own into the disappearance of Gavin Brigantz.

"This is just the tip of the iceberg," Roderick said. "There will be many more arrests forthcoming as we continue to unravel just how far-reaching this gambling ring extended across the state. Our information so far is that it's a gambling ring that Michael Boreland has been running for the better part of two years, with connections in as many as a dozen different schools."

In addition to the arrests, CHS student athlete Aaron Johnson has been expelled from the school after information came to light that he purposefully lost the school's Homecoming game against Pickering on Friday night. According to sources, the visiting Pickering team was a pre-game underdog thanks to the suspension of five of its starters, which made for lopsided betting odds in Chetfield's favor. By bribing the CHS quarterback to purposefully lose the game, Boreland was able to capitalize on the fear-based betting of those who didn't think Pickering had a chance. With his insider knowledge, Roderick said Boreland was able to make hundreds of thousands on that single game.

"We'll know more as we investigate further," Roderick said. "This is just the beginning."

CHAPTER 14

A NEW WALL CLIPPING

Chet couldn't keep the smile from his face as Dr. Delmar finished reading the story to the rest of The Scribbler staff. A picture of Gavin and Jess with an arm around each other smiled out at the class from the front page of the paper. The byline of the story included him, Kaiah, Noélle and even Justin "Chunk" Edwards, which made Chet even more happy. He was particularly proud that it had been picked up by the Associated Press and run in multiple newspapers all across the country. That was nearly unheard of for an article that originated in a student publication, let alone one written by freshmen.

"Your legend grows, Mr. Sayer," Dr. Delmar said with a wink as he lowered the paper he'd been reading from and gave Chet a little nod.

Chet looked to the side where Kaiah was sitting, and she rolled her eyes at him dramatically. He smiled at her, then glanced over at Noélle. She mimicked Kaiah almost exactly, and Chet couldn't help but laugh. When he looked at the others in the classroom, he was surprised to see many of them nodding at him with respect, and a couple of them even started clapping. Even Liz – who never seemed to smile – was looking at him with respect and a small smile.

"Aside from Mr. Sayer's excellent reporting – and you as well, Miss Dufresne and Miss Luciér – we have quite a few things to talk about," Dr. Delmar said, now addressing the entire class. "I've been quite pleased with how well we've started the year, and this story definitely will have the rest of the state looking to us to lead the way in student journalism. If we don't stand a good chance to take Best-In-State at the state newspaper awards this year then I'll eat my left shoe."

He chuckled at his own joke, but no one in the class laughed back and he cleared his throat before continuing.

"Right … well … I suppose I shouldn't count my chickens before they hatch," he said. "My point is that we've set the bar high for ourselves, and we'll have to work hard to keep up to that standard. But I daresay you all are up to the task. You'll need a new editor, however, considering your former editor is … um … no longer here."

Chet shook his head ruefully at Dr. Delmar's words and snorted softly to himself.

"Good riddance," Chet whispered to Kaiah, who blinked

at him for a moment and then gave him her winning smile and nodded in agreement.

"Liz has been doing a fantastic job as your managing editor," Dr. Delmar continued, "and it makes perfect sense to promote her to editor-in-chief. I've already spoken with her about this and she has said that she'd like Kim to serve as her managing editor."

Chet looked to the older girl who was sitting at his desk-pod and gave her a wide smile. Kim had been nice to him from the beginning, and unlike Liz she always was friendly toward people. She proved it by smiling back at him and then looked around the room at the others in the class with a slight blush on her face. Chet hoped that humility didn't mean she would be a pushover. As much as he didn't like Liz's unfriendly attitude, he whole-heartedly supported her effort to keep people accountable to deadlines. If Kim was too lax, things would fall off the rails. As if suddenly realizing the same thing, Kim's smile vanished and she gave everyone a stern look.

"Do NOT miss deadlines," she said in an exact imitation of Liz from the first day of school. "I HATE when people miss deadlines."

A brief silence was immediately followed by an eruption of laughter, and even Liz joined in after a moment. Then she stood up and turned to address the class.

"Thanks Dr. Delmar," Liz said. "I think we can all say it's been a whirlwind first couple of weeks."

Heads nodded around the room, and Chet again snorted.

"That's an understatement," he whispered to Kaiah, who shushed him.

"Things might settle down a bit, but I'd guess that we'll be following the aftermath of this story for the rest of the year," Liz said. "That means we'll need ongoing coverage of the police investigation and exposés on any teachers or administrators who are indicted. Chet, Noélle … that sounds like something you two are uniquely suited for."

Chet blinked and then smiled wide at Liz as she looked at him. She tried to keep a stern face, but the corners of her mouth twitched up and he was genuinely surprised to see fondness from her. To his left, Noélle sat up a little straighter and nodded her head with determination.

"What about me?!" Kaiah demanded, sitting up straight in her chair and staring a challenge toward Liz. Chet held his breath, hoping she wouldn't fly off the handle like she had at Sam on the first day of school. Liz just looked at her coolly before giving her a tight-lipped, but genuine, smile.

"Well … I thought you might want to tackle the parking lot story," Liz said. "If I remember right, you pointed out that the parking lot is only half full these days because of the construction. That means a lot of students aren't able to drive to school and park here – including me! If we don't have a place to park, what are we supposed to do? And why wasn't the construction finished before school started? What's the timetable for finishing the work? And isn't it a hazard to have an open construction site like that on school grounds? Also, how much did it cost? Did the school board approve only a certain amount and this project ended up going over that, and so they had to halt construction until more money was approved?"

Chet realized halfway through her barrage of questions that she was echoing everything Kaiah had said on her first day. He smiled at his friend, and she seemed taken aback but pleased by what Liz was giving her.

"Do you think you're ready for a story that big?" Liz asked, no hint of mockery in her voice.

"Yes," Kaiah squeaked, nodding her head slightly as she slunk back into her chair with a pleased smile. "Thank you."

Liz nodded to her, then turned back to the rest of the class.

"You all probably already realize this, but Caleb and Jim were the other two involved in the gambling ring and have also been suspended," Liz said. No one in the class seemed surprised by this, and she just smirked before continuing. "They were our two primary sports reporters, which leaves a very big hole on our staff in a year when we need a lot of sports coverage. So, Dr. Delmar and I have decided to recruit some promising new talent. Everyone, I'd like you to meet our new sports reporter … Justin Edwards."

Liz pointed to the door and as if on cue, Chet's best friend walked through. Chet, of course, had known about this turn of events, but he hadn't said anything to Kaiah or Noélle, and they both looked completely surprised as he walked through the door.

"Chunk!" Kaiah said, looking first to Liz, then to Chet, then back to the big football player lingering just inside the door to the room, awkwardly shuffling his feet as he tried to ignore all the eyes on him.

"That's right," Liz said thoughtfully. "Your nickname is Chunk, isn't it? Well, welcome to The Scribbler, Chunk."

The big freshman boy smiled at her, then shuffled into the room and took an open seat at a table next to Chet. Chunk seemed genuinely embarrassed, but Chet was ecstatic to have his friend as part of something that was so important to him. He shared a smile with Chunk, then turned back to Liz, who was continuing to talk.

"I've also heard that you four freshmen have come up with a name for yourselves," Liz said, looking at them curiously. "Is that right?"

Chet's face flushed as everyone's eyes turned toward them. Kaiah's face also turned a shade of red, and he was surprised to see that even Noélle seemed embarrassed by the attention. Chet reached his foot forward and nudged the back of Kaiah's seat, prompting her to give an answer. She had been the one to come up with their name, after all.

"Um … yes," Kaiah said, taking a deep breath and sitting up straight – almost defiantly, anticipating some form of belittling or laughter once she announced the name they'd come up with for themselves. "We're … um … the News Hawks."

Though a couple of people in the class did laugh, it wasn't disrespectful. In fact, most of the rest of the class nodded in approval, and Dr. Delmar was downright beaming. Liz gave them another fond smile.

"Well, News Hawks, good job," she said. "I honestly was skeptical at the beginning of the year. But you've proved me wrong. I'm anxious to see what else you come up with this year."

"Speaking of which," Noélle said, leaning forward and pulling a notepad out of her backpack. "I think we should do an exposé on the formal wear at the Homecoming dance. From what I could see this year's fashion was seriously lacking, and I think we could run a Top 10 list of the best dresses of the year. Think about how it could look with some of the pictures Dave took at the dance."

Liz just chuckled at the barrage of words from Noélle, and others in the class laughed, as well. Chet smiled warmly at her, and she hesitantly smiled back, blinking as if oblivious to her own social awkwardness.

"Before we start an official news meeting …" Dr. Delmar said suddenly, stepping forward and waving apologetically to Liz for interrupting. "There's one thing we have to do first. Mr. Sayer, would you please do the honors?"

Dr. Delmar held out a newspaper clipping, and Chet frowned at him in confusion. Dr. Delmar wiggled the clipping and then gestured toward the cork board on the wall, where the other front-page stories from years past were clipped. Chet immediately understood, and he blushed with embarrassment as he stood up quickly and grabbed the clipping from his adviser. It was, of course, the front page of The Scribbler, with the story of the missing mascot above the top fold. Chet walked proudly to the cork board, grabbed some push pins and dramatically pinned the clipping in the next open spot.

As he turned to look at his class, they broke out in applause. Chet stood there beaming as he shared smiles with his three friends.

THE END.

THE STORY CONTINUES IN ...

THE SCRIBBLER FILES:

CASE OF THE ARCHITECT'S TREASURE

Chet and his fellow News Hawks are faced with another mystery that will rock their community – but this one hits closer to home. Will Chet finally find out what his father was investigating, and more importantly, what led to his untimely and mysterious death?!

... COMING SOON!

Visit www.nudgebooks.com to join the monthly newsletter and stay up-to-date on all future book releases.

ACKNOWLEDGEMENTS

When I was a child during summer vacations my mother would start stories for me with a couple of sentences on a page and encourage me to finish those stories by the end of the day. I loved it! I never realized she was giving me the building blocks to become a storyteller. My mother planted the seed, and in many ways she deserves the first acknowledgement and my deepest gratitude for igniting the spark of a young boy's passion for great stories.

My wife has taken that ember and fanned the flame into a full-fledged reality. In September of 2019 she asked me this question: If you could do anything, what would you want to do? I didn't have to think long before I told her that I had always dreamed of being a novelist. "So do it," she said. "Make it happen." She's the one who has pushed me to tackle this dream head-on. She's the one who constantly gives me encouragement. She believes in me more than anyone else. This book – and the others that will follow after – are because of her. I can't thank her enough.

As a professional writer and editor of more than 25 years, I've come to appreciate how important it is to have a good editor – someone who can tell you when something is bad, or when there are plot holes, or when you're using far too many em dashes. Scott Firestone IV has been my go-to guy from the beginning, and his work on this book has elevated the story beyond anything I could have done on my own. I'm forever grateful for his help and expertise.

And finally, this story wouldn't exist were it not for the inspiration that came from my time as a reporter and editor for the Missouri Southern State University newspaper, The Chart. The friends I made there and the adventures I had make for some of my greatest memories. So a big thank you goes out to all of my fellow Charties.

ABOUT THE AUTHOR:

Chris Roberts is a journalist, author and all-around storyteller who makes his home in Southwest Missouri with his wife and daughter. His career started as a beat reporter for a small community newspaper and has included multiple roles as investigative reporter, editor, copywriter, graphic designer, photojournalist and even paper distributor. He's worked for nationally and globally distributed newspapers and magazines. Though his career has expanded to include scriptwriting, film-making, marketing and more, his first love is for the high calling of those beat reporters who spend their time in the trenches to shine a light on the truth. His passion is to share stories with the world that nudge people toward receptive insight. To find out more about Chris' books, please visit www.nudgebooks.com.